W9-DCZ-236

LAWRENCE '12

To Ralph From
Aunt Leana,
and Uncle
Fred.

THERE WAS NO ONE IN SIGHT, NO MOVING OBJECT ANYWHERE, AS
THE BOYS PAUSED AT THE MOUTH OF THE PASSAGE
AND GAZED ABOUT.

(Boy Scouts in California)                    (Chapter VIII)

# Boy Scouts in California

OR

## The Flag on the Cliff

By

### G. Harvey Ralphson

CHICAGO

M. A. DONOHUE & CO.

Copyright 1913
by
M. A. Donohue & Co.
CHICAGO

# CONTENTS

# Boy Scouts in California

or

## The Flag on the Cliff

### CHAPTER I

A THIEF IN THE NIGHT

"Black bear steak!"

"Grizzly bear, black bear, or cinnamon bear?"

"This is cinnamon bear! You don't suppose members of the Black Bear Patrol, Boy Scouts of America, would do a cannibal stunt by eating black bear, do you? That wouldn't be right."

Jimmie McGraw of the Wolf Patrol, City of New York, and Frank Shaw, of the Black Bear Patrol, also of New York City, were broiling bear steak over a glowing bed of embers just below the timber line on the eastern slope of the Sierra Nevada mountains. It was early morning in September, and the sunshine lay like a mist of gold over the broken country.

Away to the north rose the peaks of the Matterhorn, approximately 13,000 feet above sea level. Still nearer, Twin Peaks lifted their white heads 12,000 feet in the air. To the east lay Mono lake, salt and brackish to the taste, partaking of the desert, but bright and glistening now under the rays of the early sun.

To the south Warren Peak stood guard over the head waters of the Tuolumne river. Westward the tumbling waters of Rancheria creek dropped down from crag to crag on their winding way to the Pacific, nearly three hundred miles distant. Here and there granite peaks lifted white foreheads above the green of the pines.

It was a glorious scene, and the Boy Scouts were thoroughly in harmony with it. The smoke of their campfire lifted in a straight line to the blue of the sky, and the fragrance of their steak and coffee permeated the sweet air.

The boys shivered a trifle as they gathered closer about the embers, but they knew that before many hours the chill of the night would be swept away. While the boys tended the steak and coffee, a voice came from a cave at the rear. They both turned in that direction.

''Does this hotel serve meals to guests in their rooms?'' the voice asked.

''Sure we do!'' Jimmie McGraw replied. ''We serve grizzly bear steak on toast, and on the hoof at that; we're aiming to send you in a whole animal in about ten minutes. We feed folks right at this hotel!''

Jack Bosworth yawned sleepily and came out of the cavern to stand by the fire, warming his hands and turning round and round in order to take full advantage of the generous heat.

''Where are Ned and Harry?'' he asked in a moment.

''They've gone out to get another bear for breakfast,'' Jimmie replied. ''You see,'' he went on, ''we're getting up such appetites, here in the mountains, that it takes two hunters to keep the provison chest full.''

''After I eat,'' Jack said with a grin, ''I'm going out and bring in a deer. I'm getting tired of bear steak.''

''Go to it!'' laughed Jimmie. ''You needn't have any of this bear steak for breakfast, if you're getting sick of it.''

Jimmie and Frank each seized a huge slice of smoking steak and made for the cave, leaving Jack to broil his own breakfast in punishment for having found fault with the menu.

The cave in which the boys found themselves in a moment was not far from twenty feet in size each way, with the ceiling at least ten feet above the smooth floor. Perhaps thousands of years before that day erosion or volcanic action had honeycombed many of the granite ridges looking to the east. These openings in the ledge lay just at the timber line, as if nature halted her vegetation there, angry at the interference of contrary forces.

As the Boy Scouts had occupied the cave for several days, it was comparatively well furnished with crudely made tables, chairs, bunks, and also with cooking utensils brought up from San Francisco. Taken altogether it was an ideal place in which to camp, being dry and sightly.

Those who have read the previous volumes of this series will not need introduction to the five boys above mentioned. Ned Nestor and Jimmie McGraw, of the Wolf Patrol, New York, and Jack Bosworth, Frank Shaw and Harry Stevens, of the Black Bear Patrol, New York, had recently reached San Francisco after an exciting experience with train robbers farther to the north. The modern automobile which they had used on that trip had been shipped from Seattle to San Francisco by boat, the boys not caring to make their way by motor down to the Golden Gate.

A few days in San Francisco sufficed, for the boys were out on their annual summer vacation, and did not care to spend their time on city pavements or in city apartments. So, leaving their automobile in storage, they had departed for the mountains in the vicinity of Twin Peaks.

It is needless to say that they had enjoyed every minute of the time since leaving San Francisco. They had hunted deer, bear and smaller game, and had fished in the clear waters of the rapid streams which have their rise in the Sierra Nevadas and finally empty the offerings of the summits into San Francisco bay.

"Now, Frank," Jimmie observed as the two boys placed their still steaming steaks on paper plates set out on a table made of slender mountain poles, "you take a bucket and go after coffee and I'll bring out the bread and butter and beans. We ought to have French fried potatoes with these steaks, but I guess we can get along with this feed for a few hours. Tell Jack to come on in and eat."

Frank Shaw took a tin pail from a shelf at one side of the cave and started away toward the campfire, while Jimmie made his way to a corner of the cave which was shut off from the main room by a heavy canvas curtain. Taking a small electric flashlight from a pocket, he drew the curtain aside and turned a finger of flame upon a row of shelves arranged on the face of the rock. This was known as the "refrigerator."

Jimmie whistled as he looked over the shelves and reached out a hand, almost automatically, for the things he needed for the table. Then his puckered lips opened in wonder and he glanced sharply about the cavern.

"Well!" he exclaimed. "Now I wonder what they did that for!"

"Did what?" demanded Frank Shaw, returning with the pail of fragrant coffee. "Who did what?" repeated the newcomer.

"I believe you did it!" insisted Jimmie with a grin.

"Anything wrong with your gearing this morning?" asked Frank.

"Well," Jimmie went on, "some of you boys went and took the last three loaves of bread we had in the refrigerator, and all the butter there was in sight, and all that was left of the roast haunch we had such trouble with yesterday. I'll bet you did it!"

"Aw, you did it yourself!" exclaimed Frank. "I heard you moving around in the night, and wondered then what it was you were eating."

"Up in the night?" repeated Jimmie. "Not me!"

"Someone was out of bed in the night!" insisted Frank. "I heard someone walking around the cave and stirring up the fire. It must have been about midnight, or a little after."

"It wasn't me!" Jimmie declared, continuing

his search in the cupboard for more eatables.
"It sure wasn't me up in the night!"

After continuing his examination of the refrigerator for a moment, he handed the search
light to Frank and sat down on a corner of the
table.

"Look here, Frank," he said, "take this
search light and see if you can find anything at
all in that refrigerator. I left canned beans in
there, and condensed milk, and a tomato can
full of sugar, and about a dozen eggs! Now you
just take this light and see if you can find anything like that on the shelves. I'm flabber-
gasted!"

Frank's face showed only amusement as he
took the flashlight and threw its rays over the
rude shelves. When he saw that Jmmie had
not been joking over the disappearance of the
food, but had told the exact truth, he, too, sat
down on a corner of the table and looked about
the cavern suspiciously. When the boy's eyes
met, they grinned sheepishly.

"Go and ask Jack," Frank finally suggested.

Leaving their cooling breakfast on the table,
both boys finally dashed out of the cave and
ran around a sharp corner or rock to where Jack
Bosworth was broiling bear steak.

"Did you do it, Jack?" Frank shouted as
they came up to him.

"You bet I did!" Jack replied, turning a very red face to his chums, and drawing his now thoroughly cooked steak from the fire. "You bet I did do it. What is it?"

"How did you ever manage it?" asked Jimmie with a wrinkling of his freckled nose.

"How did I ever manage it?" repeated Jack. "What's the answer?"

Jimmie took his chum by the arm and headed for the cave.

"Bring your breakfast along with you," he said, "and hold onto it tight. Clutch it with the grip of destiny! I'll show you what I'm talking about, and then you can tell me who's got the appetite."

Directly the three boys stood before the roughly built cupboard and then Frank drew aside the canvas curtain. The shelves were entirely bare except for knives, forks, spoons, a sack of salt, and an empty plate.

"There!" Jimmie cried. "Did you go and eat all our perfectly good provender last night?"

"I wasn't out of bed last night!" insisted Jack.

"Then it must have been Ned or Harry!" Frank declared.

Jack looked from one to the other with amazement showing in his face.

"Did some one clean out the refrigerator in the night?" he asked.

"You're just right, some one cleaned out the refrigerator!" Jimmie answered, "and we've got to go and make baking powder biscuit, or corn pones, or something like that for breakfast, or go hungry!"

"I guess this bear steak will be all right for me," Jack replied. "I always did like bear steak and coffee."

"I'm not going to make any biscuit, or cook any corn pones!" Frank exclaimed. "Let the kids that robbed the refrigerator do the cooking!"

"Ned or Harry got busy in the night all right enough!" Jack insisted.

At that moment Ned Nestor and Harry Stevens, the other members of the party, entered the cavern, dressed in neat khaki uniform, as were, in fact, all the boys, and approached the table where the bear steaks lay exposed. Harry seized a knife and fork and laughingly prepared to attack Jack's breakfast. Jack seized the meat and darted out into the sunlight.

"That's a nice way to serve a guest you've invited to breakfast!" Harry exclaimed. "Where do I get my eatings this morning?"

"You and Ned got yours last night!" Jimmie grinned.

"Oh, we did?" queried Harry. "Perhaps Ned

got his last night, but if I got mine I don't know it. What are you talking about?"

"Go and look in the refrigerator," suggested Jimmie.

Both Ned and Harry walked to the corner and drew aside the curtain. They stood in front of the empty shelves for a moment, and then walked back to the table, their faces showing only amusement.

"What did you do with it?" asked Ned, presently, as Jimmie and Frank attacked their fast-cooling steaks vigorously.

"What did *you* do with it?"

Frank answered the question by asking one.

Ned Nestor's face became serious in a moment. He glanced from one chum to the other, and then went to the shelves and looked them over thoroughly. There was a puzzled line between his eyebrows as he walked back and seated himself beside Jimmie and Frank.

"Honest, now, boys," he asked, "what does this all mean?"

"Didn't you get the eatings?" asked Jimmie seriously.

"I certainly did not!" replied Nestor, seriously.

"Now about you, Harry?" Jimmie questioned. "Where did you find a market for all that good provender?"

"Never touched it!" Harry insisted. "I went to bed at nine o'clock, as you all know, and when I awoke the sun was just showing his nose over the foothills."

"And you were good and hungry, too, just about that time!" Jimmie scoffed. "You must have been hungry to eat all that!"

"Wait a minute, boys," Ned replied. "There's something mysterious about this! No wild animal ever entered the cave last night. Some creature on two legs stripped the refrigerator while we slept!"

"Je-rusalem!" exclaimed Jimmie. "It's a wonder he didn't do something more than steal our grub."

"I didn't suppose," Frank cut in, "that there was a human being anywhere in this district except ourselves."

"Well," Ned replied, "there's some one prowling about, and the thing for us to do is to find out who it is."

"It's the mystery of the thing that gets me!" declared Frank.

## CHAPTER II

### A VOICE IN THE THICKET

"That's just what it is—a mystery!" Jimmie McGraw exclaimed.

"How could anyone get in here and lug away a load of provisions like that without our waking up? They just couldn't do it!"

This from Jack, who had now returned with his half-eaten steak.

"I heard some one moving around in the night," Frank declared.

"Then, why didn't you get up and see about it?" asked Ned.

"Oh, I thought I dreamed it!" grinned Frank.

"I'd give a good deal to know who it was that had the nerve to pay us a visit in the night-time," Ned said, presently. "I don't like the idea of keeping open house during the dark hours. The person who came here last night may come again, and may make more trouble the next time."

"And that means," Jimmie complained, "that we've got to set a guard every night, and watch our property, just like we were on Third Avenue in New York. It makes me sick to think of it!"

"And just think of all the fun we've been having here, playing that we were scores of miles away from anybody!  Look here, boys," he went on, "we've been under the sea and over the sea.  We've had adventures in Panama and in China, and I don't think we ever had anyone walk over our sleeping forms and steal provisions before."

"That's right!" Frank answered.  "We must be getting careless in our old age.  Now the next thing is to find out who did this."

"Some poor tramp, probably," suggested Ned.  "We'll make a business of watching for him during the next few hours, and probably we'll catch him.  I'm sure I hope it was a tramp, for I don't want to get mixed up with any hostile element up here."

As Ned ceased speaking he went to the rough cupboard again and began a second inspection of the shelves.  Newspapers had been neatly arranged on the boards, and these did not appear to have been disturbed.  After going over everything in sight thoroughly, the boy took the sack of salt out to the open sunlight and examined it critically.

"Now, Mr. Sherlock Holmes, what do you find there?" demanded Frank.  "I'll tell you what," he went on, "we have seemed to forget that Dad owns one of the leading newspapers in

New York City! I will sit down right now and write a long article and call it 'The Magic Breakfast; or, Who Stole the Beans!' I think that title would make a hit on the Bowery, eh?''

''It's about time you began sending in correspondence,'' Jimmie grinned. ''You know you promised to send in a full account of our ruction with the train robbers, but you never did. The first thing you know, your father will be cutting off your supply of ready cash.''

''Oh, well, then,'' Frank laughed, ''I'll retain Jack's father, who is a rich corporation lawyer, and sue Dad for a breach of promise, or something like that. But look at Ned,'' the boy went on, ''he's surely found something on that salt sack!''

''Is that right, Sherlocko, you Sleuth?'' asked Jimmie.

Ned turned to his chums with amusement showing in his eyes.

''Let me read you the story told by the salt sack,'' he said whimsically. ''And remember,'' he went on, as the boys laughed and nudged each other, ''this story will not be reprinted in book form, so you'll have to catch it as I tell it. It will not even be told again!''

''Go on with your blessed old dope,'' laughed Frank.

''Well,'' Ned began, holding the sack up for

inspection, "the person who stole our provisions took salt from this sack in order to season his meal. He took quite a lot, too, judging from the way the salt lowered during the night. Probably thought he'd take enough while the taking was good, for which we can't blame him."

"We knew all that before!" Jimmie declared.

"Now listen," Ned went on, "here comes the magic part of the case! The person who took the salt from this sack was fifteen years of age. He was tall and slender, and had gone without food for three days. He did not come down from the divide, but crept up from the valley. He was lightly clad, and wore a ragged coat and broken shoes. He stood outside the cave for a long time before gaining courage to enter."

The boys gathered around Ned with laughing faces and pretended to inspect the salt bag with reverential interest.

"Go on, now," Jimmie demanded. "Go on and give us the answer to all this! Tell us how you know so much about a person you have never seen."

"Look here," Ned explained, "I know the person was a boy because the finger marks on the sack show a small, slender hand. Slender fingers represent a slender body, you know, and that's why I say the person was young and slim."

"That's good deduction!" Frank declared. "Now tell us how you know that he hadn't had anything to eat for three days."

"Look at the shelves and you'll discover how I know for yourselves," Ned said, marching the boys into the back end of the cave.

"You will notice," he went on, "that the shelf where the bread lay is covered with crumbs. That shows that he began to eat the minute his hands touched the loaf. He must have been perfectly ravenous to begin his meal while in such imminent danger of discovery. Of course, he might have dined in less than three days, but I think he'd have to be pretty hungry in order to eat with five boys likely to wake up at any moment lying around him. You see that, don't you?"

"That's good, too!" Jack exclaimed. "Now, how do you know whether he came down the slope to the timber line or up the slope from the valley?"

"If you notice the floor directly in front of the shelves," Ned explained pointing, "you will see numerous pine leaves scattered about. Now, there are no pines above the cavern, so the boy crawled through the thickets below. Is that clear?"

"Clear as mud!" shouted Frank, "and suppose you have got a photograph of him so that you know that he was ragged and wore broken shoes!"

"Look at the nail sticking out of the shelf," Ned went on, "and you'll see several shreds of cloth hanging to it. Jack thought he was making a pretty good job on that cupboard but he left a nail sticking up, just the same. The nail tells the story of a ragged sleeve."

"Correct!" laughed Jimmie. "Now, how are you going to make good on the broken shoes?" he continued.

"That's the easiest part of it all," Ned answered. "When he stood in the cool ashes close to the embers, he left imprints of wornout soles."

The boys broke into shouts of laughter and Frank declared that he would immortalize Ned as a detective in his father's newspaper.

"Yes, but hold on!" Jack interposed. "Did you hold a stop watch on him while he stood outside the cave, Ned?"

"He held a stop watch on himself," the boy answered. "You can see where he walked about, taking many steps and stirring up the wash from the rocks at the mouth of the cave. Now do you understand?"

"Now, then," Jimmie questioned, "perhaps you can tell us where this boy is, and why he didn't make himself known to us if he was as hungry as you say he was. Go on, now, and tell!''

''And while you're about it,'' Jack suggested, ''you might as well tell us whether the boy who stole our grub is white or black or mixed.''

''There are limits to the ability of even a Sherlock Holmes,'' laughed Ned, ''but,'' he continued, more seriously, ''there is little doubt that the person who stole our provisions is just about as I have described him.''

The boys now gathered about the fire again, and Ned and Harry proceeded to broil steaks for their breakfast. After a time Jimmie and Frank wandered down into the pines in the hope of securing the material for a squirrel stew for a dinner.

It was still and dim in the thicket except for the ceaseless murmur of the trees. The sun's rays could not penetrate the heavy foliage. Here and there great rocks, evidently shunted down from the summits in some convulsion of nature, lay scattered about.

''Talk about your weird places,'' Jimmie exclaimed, ''this beats any graveyard I ever saw!''

''That's no dream!'' Frank answered. ''I've been hearing ghostly voices for the last ten minutes. Listen, and you will hear them, too!''

Before the words were well out of the boy's

mouth, Jimmie caught him by the arm and drew him to the shelter of a great tree.

"What did you say about ghostly voices? he asked.

"Aw, that was just a joke!" Frank replied.

"But I did actually hear some one speak!" Jimmie insisted.

"If you heard anything at all it was a bear, or a deer, or a squirrel or something like that!" Frank declared. "Just you wait a minute and see if you don't hear some bear ordering us off his premises."

While the boys stood close to the bole of a pine, listening, a shrill, excited voice came to them from some undiscoverable quarter.

At first they could not distinguish the words which were spoken. Jimmie turned to his chum with a half frightened grin on his face.

"Does that sound like bear-talk?" he asked.

"Not a bit of it!" Frank admitted, "but it may be one of the boys playing a joke on us. They are full of such tricks."

Then the voice came to their ears again, lifted just above the sighing of the pines—sharp, imperative.

"Beat it! Beat it!"

The two boys gazed into each other's faces with wonder in their eyes.

"Can you beat that?" Jimmie asked. "Was that a bear?"

Again the words of warning came to the ears of the amazed boys:

"Beat it while the going is good!"

"That sounds like Second avenue!" Jimmie ventured.

Frank turned in the direction from whence the sound had seemed to proceed and called out:

"What's your motto?"

"Be prepared!" was the answer that came back.

"Be prepared for what?" demanded Jimmie.

"To help a friend!" was the answer.

"Look here!" Jimmie shouted. "If you're a Boy Scout, why don't you come out and show yourself? I never knew a Boy Scout who was ashamed to show his face."

"What patrol?" came the voice from the thicket.

"Black Bear and Wolf, New York," Frank answered.

There was a short silence, and then just a whisper came from a point near to where the boys were standing.

"Didn't I tell you Boy Scouts to beat it?" were the words spoken.

"What's the difficulty?" asked Jimmie. "Are

you trying to make monkeys of us?   Why don't you come out and tell us all about it?''

''It wouldn't do any good if I did,'' answered the mysterious voice. ''I tell you to beat it, and that's the last word you'll get from me.''

They heard a rustle in the thicket, and, though they listened for a long time, they heard no more words spoken. The boys darted away into the undergrowth in search of the person who had given them so mysterious a warning, but no trace of him could be discovered.

''Now, what did he mean by 'beat it'?'' demanded Jimmie in a moment as the boys met at the tree again.

''He meant for us to make ourselves scarce in this vicinity, I'm afraid,'' Frank answered. ''Of course we don't know whether he warned us to keep away from this spot, or whether he advised us to break camp.''

''If he thinks we're going to break camp on any bum old steer like that,'' Jimmie grumbled, ''he's got several more thinks coming.''

''Anyway,'' laughed Frank, ''we wouldn't feel just right unless we got into some kind of a mysterious situation. We've never been out on a trip that we didn't butt into something desperate and uncanny.''

After another investigation of the locality, the boys hastened back to camp.   They were met by Harry and Jack, who regarded them with inquiring eyes, seeming to be astonished by their return.

"Where's Ned?" Jack finally asked.

"Why, we left him here," both boys replied in a breath.

"Of course," Harry returned, "but you sent a line asking him to come to where you were. What did you go and do that for if you were coming right back to camp? Was that a joke?"

"Joke nothing!" Jimmie answered. "We never sent any such word!"

"Then who sent that strange note?" Jack asked. "I'll bet we're up against something mighty serious right now!"

## CHAPTER III

### THE LAW OF CLUB AND FANG

"Where's the note?" asked Frank.

"It isn't here," Harry answered, "so I guess Ned must have taken it with him. He had it the last time I saw it."

"What kind of a note was it?"

"Just a short note written on letter paper in pencil."

"Well, what did it say?"

"It said for Ned to come to where you were, and leave the others in camp. You say you never sent it?"

"Of course, we never sent it!" replied Jimmie scornfully. "We don't carry paper and pencil with us every time we leave camp!"

"Who brought it?" Frank cut in.

"Why, a dark-skinned little chap who said he had left you in a gulch not far away."

"Did he look like the boy Ned described this morning?" asked Jimmie.

"Come to think of it, I guess he did!" answered Jack. "Anyway, he was a ragged little chap and looked hungry."

"Hungry after eating three or four loaves

of bread and a lot of canned beans!" grinned Frank. "Did Ned go away with him?"

"Of course, he went away with him."

"Then there's some deviltry afloat," Frank declared. "Some one out there in the thicket told us to 'beat it while the beating was good,' and then ducked away. I'll bet it was the same person."

In answer to numerous questions, Jimmie and Frank related their experience in the pines.

"Now, what are we going to do about it?" asked Harry with a troubled look on his face. "There certainly is mischief afoot."

"The first thing to do," Jack replied, "is to scatter and see if we can find Ned. He's been lured away, and may be in trouble."

"We're the original trouble-getters!" Harry grumbled. "I believe we'd get into a mixup of some kind if we went to a Sunday School picnic.

"And the strangest part of it all is," Frank went on, "that the boy who told us to 'beat it' proved to be a Boy Scout!"

"Anyway," Jimmie declared, "he answered our challenge correctly."

While the boys consulted together, anxious for the safety of their chum, a shout came from the summit above.

"There's something new," Jimmie grinned.

"I wonder whether that fellow wants bread and beans, or whether he wants to coax one of us away into the woods? Tell him this is our busy day!"

"Are you there, boys?" came the voice from above.

"Hello yourself!" Jimmie called back.

"All right, now," the voice went on. "All I needed was something to enable me to locate you. I'll be down there in a minute."

"That'll be nice!" Jimmie answered. "If you've got a trunk full of trouble, just bring that along with you. We're in the market for trouble."

Although the boys made light of the approach of another visitor, they were very anxious. They were certain that Ned had been lured away for some sinister purpose, and were consequently fearful that this new arrival might be connected in some way with future complications.

In a few moments rolling stones and exclamations of impatience announced the near approach of the man who had hailed them. Directly he turned around an angle of rock and came into full view.

He was a short, fat, heavily built man of perhaps thirty, with the pale face and assertive manner of a city dweller. At all events it was plainly evident that he was not familiar with mountain work, for he stumbled about as he advanced down the declivity, and more than once fell to his knee and caught hold of projecting boulders with a pair of hands not at all familiar with such service.

Jack eyed the fellow critically for a moment, and then advanced to meet him with a shout of welcome.

"Gilroy!" he cried. "What the Old Harry are you doing away out in California? Boys," he continued, turning to his chums, "this is Gilroy, one of Dad's confidential clerks. Nothing wrong at home, I hope," he continued addressing the newcomer.

"All were well and happy when I left New York," Gilroy returned, puffing with his long struggle with the mountain side.

"Did Dad give you a vacation?" asked Jack.

"Vacation nothing!" Gilroy answered. "He sent me flying over the continent on a special train, and told me to get to you in seven days. This is the tenth day I've been on the road."

"Whew!" whistled Jack. "Dad won't like that."

"I'm sorry, but I can't help it," Gilroy returned. "Your father measured surface distances only. He didn't figure how many thousands of miles I'd have to go up in the air in order to find you!"

"It is some climb," Jack admitted, "but what's the rush?"

"If you've got a place here where we can talk without being in danger of being overheard," Gilroy suggested, "I'll tell you all about it."

"Oh you can say whatever you have to say in the presence of my chums," Jack answered. "They won't leak."

"That isn't the idea," Gilroy stated. "Your father even instructed me to report to your chums if you were not to be found. I know the boys are all right, but the fact is that he is afraid of rank outsiders."

"Rank outsiders!" repeated Jack with a laugh. "Who is there up here on the mountain to listen to private conversation? Eavesdroppers couldn't get within sound of our voices without being seen if they tried."

"They couldn't, eh?" Harry cut in. "They couldn't get close enough to steal our beans, or to tell you boys to beat it while the beatin' was good, or to send a fake note in order to get hold of Ned!"

"What's that you say?" asked Gilroy. "Has Ned Nestor already been lured away?"

"He certainly has!" answered Jimmie. "While Frank and I were away a strange boy brought a note and Ned fell for it."

"And some one stole your provisions, too?" the fat clerk asked.

"Stole everything last night that wasn't locked up in the provisions boxes," answered Harry.

"And appeared to us in the bushes and told us to beat it," put in Jimmie. "I wonder if he did that before he brought that lying note to Ned? Oh, we seem to be keeping busy all right!"

"Why," Frank suggested, "he must have seen us before he brought the note, for he went away with Ned."

Gilroy looked very much puzzled for a moment and then said:

"I'm afraid that this is a scheme to get Nestor out of the way. If I could only have reached you on schedule time, this would never have happened. Still, I did the best I could under the circumstances."

"I hope you also didn't come out here to tell us to 'beat it,'" laughed Frank. "We've just got to enjoying ourselves."

"I came out to deliver a message from Mr. Bosworth," Gilroy answered. "He has some work he wants you boys to do."

"Work is right in our line!" Harry answered with a laugh.

"Well, hurry up and tell us all about it,"

Jack suggested calmly, ''because, you know, we ought to be out looking for Ned.''

''It's just this way,'' Gilroy began, ''Jack's father is acting as attorney for a large mining corporation. His employers have always believed their title to certain lands in this vicinity absolutely flawless. Some of these lands are valuable for timber, some for minerals, and some for agricultural purposes. As I said before, some of these lands lie in this vicinity, and a railroad the employers own will soon build a spur in here to market the minerals and the lumber.

''Now,'' the confidential clerk went on, ''it has been discovered that there are other claimants to these lands. It is asserted that they were given to the descendants of Franciscan monks who were here at the time so many missions were scattered over California. At any rate, people who came over with the Franciscans, if not Franciscans themselves, left progeny who now claim these lands.

''The Mexican government recognized the titles, but the United States government never did. The claimants have no standing whatever in the courts, but they propose to keep possession under the old law of club and fang. Of course, they can't keep possession long, but they can put the corporation to a great deal of trouble."

"It looks to me," Jack interrupted with a grin, "that father should have sent a regiment of United States troops instead of one confidential clerk. Now, just what is it he wants us to do?"

"He wants you boys to scout about and find out exactly who is at the bottom of all this trouble. He believes that the alleged heirs are ignorant pawns in the hands of a corporation with which his own companies are at sword's points.

"His first thought was to send a company of detectives in here, but he concluded later on that a vacation crowd of Boy Scouts would attract less attention, and might not be suspected at all. In accordance with this reasoning he sent me out to tell you to learn everything possible regarding present complications."

"Does he think this corporation he is fighting has already sent mercenaries out here to make trouble?" asked Jack.

"He is quite positive that such is the case," answered Gilroy. "At any rate, he wants you to find out what kind of people they have leading this outlaw gang."

"I knew it would come," Jack laughed.

"Every time we go out for a vacation, we get mixed up in a scrap of some kind."

"Well," Frank suggested, "we have all the more fun because of the trouble we get into. I like to be doing things."

"But how are we going to get a line on these people?" asked Jack.

"It seems to me that they've got in the first blow," Harry declared. "If we only had Ned here, he could tell us exactly what to do."

"We'll have him here before night!" Jimmie answered.

"You ask how you are to get a line on the people you are to watch," Gilroy said, "and I think I can tell you what you ought to do first. It is said that somewhere out in the hills, perhaps within a few miles of this very spot, there are the ruins of an old Franciscan mission. It is said to stand high up on a mountain, facing east. Our information is that the walls of the original mission have been leveled to the ground, but that the subterranean rooms and passages reaching under the mountain are still fairly intact. You must find this mission."

"And after we find it, what then?" Jack asked.

"It is said to be the headquarters of the outlaw claimants who are making us all this trouble," replied Gilroy. "If you find the ruined mission, you will also find, without

doubt, the agents of the corporation we are fighting.   They are undoubtedly there.''

''And after we find them, what then?'' Frank
questioned.

''What Mr. Bosworth wants,'' the confidential clerk continued, ''is to connect this
hostile corporation, through its agents, with
what is going on here.   Once in the possession
of positive information that the corporation is
instigating this revolt against law and order,
and he will know exactly what to do.   He ex-
pects you boys to bring in the proof.''

''Are you going to remain and help us?''
asked Jack in a moment.

''Remain and help you?'' repeated the fat
little confidential clerk in dismay.   ''I should
say not!   In fact, Mr. Bosworth was thoughtful
enough to intimate to me that I would better
get out of the mountains as soon as possible
after delivering my message. Personally, I
wouldn't stay in these hills for a thousand dollars
a day!''

''If you'll wait until we find this romantic
old mission,'' Jack grinned, ''we'll make you a
suite of rooms that will beat anything in New
York.''

''Say, boys,'' Gilroy answered with a grim
smile, ''I'd rather be blind and be tied to a lamp

post in New York than to own all the country west of the Mississippi river."

"Well, then," Jack said, "run back to Dad with your little old story about Ned's being abducted the day you reached us!"

"If you do," Jimmie called out, "we'll murder you when we get back to New York! Ned will be with us before you get down to the foot-hills."

"I certainly hope so," Gilroy answered.

"Because," Jimmie declared, "we're going out right now to find that romantic old mission and dig him out of a ruined chamber!"

## CHAPTER IV

### JIMMIE BUILDS TWO FIRES

"I am really alarmed about the disappearance of Mr. Nestor," Gilroy said, as the boys began frying ham and eggs and making fresh coffee for him. "There is no doubt at all in my mind that he was induced to leave the camp by the agents of the hostile corporation."

"No doubt about that," Jimmie put in.

"And that means," Gilroy went on, "that they really suspect what you are here for. That is the worst part of it."

"But why should they suspect us?" demanded Jimmie. "We never knew a thing about the complications until you came in here half an hour ago!"

"I'll tell you why they're suspicious of us," Jack exclaimed. "They know that I am the son of the lawyer who is putting up the fight against them. Now you see how the case stands! We've been given a mission to execute on the theory that we could work without being suspected, when, as a matter of fact, we were suspected before we were given the work to do."

"That's funny!" Jimmie laughed.

"It might be humorous if it wasn't so serious," the confidential clerk explained, pompously, "and I'm going to give you boys a little advice, which may not meet with the approval of Jack's father."

"Go to it!" laughed Jack.

"This hostile corporation," Gilroy continued, "will, in my opinion, stop at nothing in order to accomplish their ends. Now that the unexpected has happened—now that their agents suspect that you are here to watch and, if possible, frustrate their designs—my advice is that you get out of the country as quickly as possible."

"And leave Ned here?" demanded Jimmie scornfully.

"If you boys break camp and leave the mountains at once," Gilroy advised, "the agents of the corporation will not hold Nestor for any great length of time. Nestor, as you boys well know, has an international reputation for clever work in the detective line. Still, it is well known, that he works with Boy Scouts invariably, and the people who have abducted him will understand that he would be likely to abandon any case not shared with his old chums. Am I right in that?"

"You've got it sized up right!" declared Jimmie.

"I wonder why they didn't trap me?" Jack asked.

"I rather wonder at that, too," Gilroy answered.

"Huh," laughed Frank. "They wanted the detective, and not the son of his father. To capture Jack would be to admit that their efforts were directed against the corporations under the control of Mr. Bosworth."

"Well," the confidential clerk insisted, "I am certain that, under the circumstances, Mr. Bosworth would object to your remaining here on any errand of his. For my own part, I advise you to get out of the mountains as soon as possible."

"And miss all this fun?" demanded Jimmie with a grin.

"But I insist that you boys are in deadly peril here!" Gilroy went on. "Urged on by the agents of this hostile corporation, there is no knowing what desperate measures these outlaws claimants may resort to. But if you insist on remaining here against my advice, and against the advice your father would give if he understood the circumstances, you ought to move your camp to some place not in the knowledge of the outlaws. You can at least do that."

"What's the use?" asked Jack. "Don't you suppose they've got people watching us now?

From this time on, we can't make a move without their knowing it. We may as well stay here and barricade this cave.''

''That's a good idea!'' Jimmie exclaimed. ''All we've got to do is to roll a few large boulders down the slope and line them up at the entrance of the cavern. We'll be as snug as bugs in a rug in behind them, and we have provisions enough to last us for a month.''

''Yes,'' Harry submitted, ''and we can lay behind the boulders and shoot outlaws and railroad mercenaries to our hearts' content!''

''Its dangerous, boys, its dangerous!'' insisted Gilroy.

''Huh, we're just beginning to enjoy ourselves, now that we have some object in life!'' Jimmie insisted.

The boys set to work with a vim rolling boulders down the slope and placing them in front of the cave. It was the work of only a few minutes to barricade the entire entrance to within a foot of the top, leaving only a narrow place to pass in and out. Thus protected, the cave was quite dark but the electric flashlights carried by the boys would, they considered, supply sufficient illumination.

''And now,'' Jimmie said, regarding the work critically, ''we can give our whole attention to learning what has become of Ned.''

"If you don't mind, boys," Gilroy interrupted, "I wish you'd give a little attention to the ham and eggs and coffee you are preparing for my breakfast! This mountain air creates an appetite."

"Sure thing!" Harry shouted. "We forgot all about your breakfast, and there's the ham burning and the coffee bubbling over. But just you wait a minute," he went on, "and we'll soon have a meal better than any you could get at the Waldorf-Astoria!"

While the breakfast was being cooked and eaten, Gilroy continued to urge the boys to go out with him and wait at the nearest transportation point for Ned to follow them. The boys only laughed at the idea, however, and ended by urging him to remain with them until Ned should be brought back.

"I'll tell you what I'll do, boys," the confidential clerk finally stated, "if you'll give me a big roll of blankets and leave someone on watch, I'll go back in the cave and sleep for about three days. Do you think you can find your detective friend in that time?"

"In three days?" laughed Jack. "We'll be able to send you back to father in less time with a full report as to what is doing in the mountains."

"I hope you're right," Gilroy said.

He turned toward the barricaded cave but halted at the very entrance.

"What was it you said," he asked, "about the boy who warned you in the thicket being a Boy Scout?"

"He answered the challenge all right," replied Frank.

"If he really is a Boy Scout," asked Gilroy tentatively, "he ought to be loyal to his comrades, don't you think?"

"Yes, he ought to be," Jack answered, "but then, you know, there are renegades in all grades and ranks of society.   Still, this boy may have been acting under compulsion."

"I have read a great deal about Boy Scouts being loyal to each other," Gilroy continued, "and I can't help thinking that this one will in time do something to make amends for his seemingly hostile act in delivering a fraudulent note.   I have faith in the Boy Scout league!"

"And so have we all of us!" declared Jack. "We have found Boy Scouts in all parts of the world, and we have always found them loyal and trustworthy.   This lad may yet prove to be so."

"Why," Jimmie interrupted, "he did show that he was made of the right kind of stuff when he took the pains to follow us into the forest and advise us to get out of the country."

"Yes," Jack laughed, "but he returned from that excursion and delivered a lying note to Ned. Still," the boy went on more mildly, "we don't know anything about the circumstances surrounding the matter, so we'll give him the benefit of every doubt."

"I only made the suggestion," Gilroy advised, "in order that you boys might be looking for some indication of friendliness on the part of this seeming enemy. The boy may be of great use to you yet."

"It's a mystery to me how they ever got a true Boy Scout mixed up in a dirty game!" Harry declared. "This boy is no easy mark. The language he used said 'New York' just as plain as anything, so they must have brought him clear from the big city for some purpose of their own."

"Well," Gilroy said in a moment, "I've given you the best advice I have at my command, and made what I regard as a valuable suggestion," he continued with a laugh, "and now I'll go to bed and dream that I'm back in New York sleeping on top of the Singer building."

"The Singer building ain't nothing to this," Harry grinned, sweeping his hand over the great stretch of country to the east. "From the top of the Singer building you can't see the back yard of half a dozen states."

Gilroy passed through the narrow opening and the four boys gathered about the fire to lay plans for the future.

"Now, whatever we do," Frank suggested, "we must never leave this cave unprotected. Just as long as we have a bullet proof place to hide away in, and plenty of provisions, they can't drive us out of the mountains with anything less than a piece of artillery. They know exactly where to find us, so we won't have to go chasing through the woods looking for them!" he added with a grin.

"That'll help some!" Harry laughed, "especially when we want to sleep and have to set up to dodge bullets."

"There ain't going to be no bullets!" laughed Jack.

"And now," Jimmie suggested, "I'm going to take a little stroll for my health. I'm afraid I'm not getting sufficient exercise."

"Before we turn him loose in the mountains," Jack laughed, "we ought to tie a bell on him. Jimmie has a way of getting lost that approaches the artistic. I believe he'd get lost in a hall bedroom."

"Perhaps I'd better go with him," Harry ventured.

"No you won't!" Jimmie said. "I'm going out alone, and I'm going to c-r-e-e-p and c-r-e-e-p and c-r-e-e-p through the bushes like one of J. Fennimore Cooper's forresters.''

"Robin Hood would have been stuck on you!" grinned Frank.

"You bet he would!" Jimmie insisted gravely. "Me and Robin Hood would have had some great times together in Lincoln forest."

"Go on, then, you little runt!" Jack exclaimed. "Go on and get back as soon as possible, for we're all anxious to get on the hunt for Ned."

Jimmie laughed and disappeared in the pines lower down on the slope. He walked steadily to the east and north for, perhaps, half an hour and then began a series of operations which even his friends might not have understood at the beginning.

Stopping at the foot of a granite finger which thrust a broad surface half way up to the tops of the pines, he began gathering dry boughs. After a great heap had been secured, he carried them with great exertion to the top of the elevation. It was necessary for him to make several trips up and down the steep side of the rock but at last two great heaps of perfectly dry boughs lay on the hard surface of the cliff.

One more trip to the bottom he made, to return with a great back load of green pine boughs. Then he sat down, panting, and regarded his work with no little satisfaction.

"I don't know," he mused, wiping the perspiration from his forehead, "but I ought to climb one of these trees. I'd do it, too, only I'm afraid I couldn't get the fires into line on the boughs."

He heaped the dry boughs into neat, compact array and then covered them heavily with the green branches. This done, he set fire to each of the two piles and sat down to await results.

The flames ate fast into the dry faggots and the green boughs above made such a white smudge as had rarely been seen in that vicinity.

"There," the boy mused, "there's two towering columns of smoke! In Indian talk, they mean 'I want some one to come and help me out of a mess,' and that is what the two smudges say in Boy Scout language, too. Now I wonder if anyone save the lads at the camp will see and understand. I hope the kids at the cave will recognize this as an invitation to the bearer of the note alone, and not directed to themselves."

The two columns of smoke ascended straight into the sky for perhaps ten minutes and then died down. Jimmie sat at the top of the rock and waited. The forest around him seemed alive with creeping and flying things, and sunshine filtered softly through the branches of the great pines. After a time he climbed to the top of a great tree and looked over the landscape.

To the south and west he saw the faint column of smoke lifting from the campfire. To the north and west mountain peaks lifted above the range, many of them white with snow.

''Now,'' the boy mused, ''unless the messenger is shut up, or tied up, or rendered motionless by the muzzle of a gun, I ought to know before very long whether he is a good Boy Scout or a renegade.''

## CHAPTER V

### THE CALL OF THE PACK

From his high perch in the tree Jimmie could see far above the timber line and clearly distinguish slopes, ledges and precipitous canyons invisible as a whole to one walking on the surface, or even one looking down from a high cliff on the mountains themselves. To the north a snow-covered summit glistened in the sun, the great white cloak unbroken at the top but showing bare spaces farther down.

Looking in wonder and awe at this magnificent manifestation of nature, Jimmie began to realize, dimly, that the lines of snow on the lower stretches of the mountain seemed to lie at one point parallel with each other. It was as if trenches had been dug in the form of a parallelogram and the excavations filled in with snow.

The outline was so distinct that the boy regarded it curiously for a long time. It seemed to him that the hand of the Snow King had sketched on the mountainside a plan for a structure which had never been built.

Just above the spot where this remarkable pattern lay was a precipice fifty or more feet in height. This wall seemed to the boy to be absolutely vertical. There was a shelf of rock below the strange snow-line, and beneath that the heavy slope of the range.

Turning his eyes at last from the snow-covered summits, the boy gazed eagerly over the forest to left and right, studying the landscape for some indication of a signal. Directly he saw the column of smoke arising from the campfire strengthening into a black mass, and knew that the boys were answering his call not knowing by whom it had been sent forth. He smiled whimsically as he turned his eyes away.

''That tells me where the camp is, anyway!'' he laughed.

Five minutes later, just as the boy was about to descend from his tree, he caught sight of the signal for which he had been waiting. Two columns of smoke arose from a point on the timber line near strange snow formation which he had been considering.

''There's our Boy Scout!'' he declared, scrambling quickly to the ground.

Once out of the tree, the boy made no haste in approaching the spot from which the signal had come. Instead of proceeding in a direct line he turned down the slope and walked swiftly to the north.

Half an hour's steady traveling brought him

to a point almost directly east of the columns of smoke. He could not see the smoke at all now, but knew of its location by the snow-capped cliff almost in front of which it had lifted. After reaching this point he walked directly west.

It was no easy matter, climbing the rugged side of the mountain, but the boy persisted in his work until at last he came to a shelf of rock which seemed to be not far away from where the signals had been shown. Stopping to rest, he looked toward the camp for some indication of further activity in the way of signals there but none came.

The campfire itself, and the face of rock into which the cave had long ago been cut, were not in sight from the point where he stood, the timber line creeping up in the form of an inverted "V" and shutting out all that portion of the lower level to the south.

Just as the boy was about to proceed, the long, snarling, vicious call of a wolf came from a thicket not far away. The boy involuntarily drew his automatic revolver and stepped behind the bole of a giant pine.

In a moment the call came again and again.

There was a note in it which seemed to the boy to speak of human lips. While he listened another call—louder, longer, more insistent—

came—the call of the pack! Jimmie almost danced in his excitement.

"The Wolf Patrol!" he shouted. "The good old Wolf Patrol!"

Throwing back his head he produced an excellent imitation of the challenge he had heard. It echoed through the forest singly for a moment and was then joined by the call which had attracted his attention.

"Mother of Moses!" the boy cried. "The people will think there's a whole pack of timber wolves in the country.

Advancing now through the thicket, the boy soon saw a motion in the underbrush not far away. He stood still and waited.

"Hello, Wolf!" he shouted in a moment.

"Hello, Wolf!" came the answer.

"Show your colors!" Jimmie called.

In a moment a slender, dusky boy advanced out of the thicket and approached Jimmie, his right hand extended palm out, thumb and little finger crossed—the full sign of the Boy Scout.

Jimmie sat flat down on the ground his back against a tree trunk and regarded the lad quizzically.

"You the kid that brought that note?" he asked.

The other nodded, and Jimmie went on with a mock air of censure.

"What'd you do it for?" he demanded.

"Aw, what's all this?" said the other scornfully.

"The third degree," Jimmie grinned. What'd you bring that note for? Now you've gone and got Ned Nestor into trouble. What's your name?" he continued as the boy bent his face to the ground.

"Norman," was the reply, "Wolf Patrol, New York."

"You're a new one on me!" asserted Jimmie. "I belong to the Wolf Patrol, New York. Never saw you before!"

"You're Jimmie McGraw?" Norman asked.

"How do you know that?"

"On account of your nerve!" Norman answered.

"What're you going to do about it?" asked Jimmie belligerently.

"I've been ordered," Norman went on with a smile, "to break you in two if I came across you in the mountains."

"Do it, then!" shouted Jimmie. "You've gone and got Ned into a mess, and I'd just like to have you try something on me now!"

Instead of showing temper, Norman sat down on the ground and laughed until he felt obliged to hold his sides.

"How'd you ever get away out here in the

mountains?'' Jimmie asked.  ''Ain't you afraid you'll get lost?''

''I haven't got lost yet!'' was the scornful reply.

''Come now,'' Jimmie said, in a more conciliating tone of voice, ''put me wise to the game you're playing with Nestor.''

''All I know about it is that I delivered the note.''

''Where is Nestor?''

''I left him talking with a very fine gentleman who seemed to be offering to do the square thing with him,'' was the reply.

''Bribing him, was he?''

''I don't know about that.  He was offering him money.''

''When will Nestor return to camp?'' asked Jimmie.

Norman shook his head gravely.

''Do you mean that they won't let him go?'' demanded the boy.

''I don't know anything about it,'' Norman answered.

''Who told you to rope Ned into such a mess?''

''The man I work for.''

''What's his name?'' asked Jimmie then.

''His name is Toombs,'' was the reply.  ''He hired me to come out on a hunting trip with him and help around the camp.''

"How many are there in the party?" was Jimmie's next question.

"Only two, Toombs and a black looking heathen named Huga. I guess he's an Indian. Anyway, he's a mighty evil-looking fellow."

"Well," Jimmie announced accusingly, "those fellows are not out here on a hunting trip at all! They're out here to make trouble for Ned Nestor and his friends. I think you've done a mighty cute trick in helping them along with their work!"

"Say," Norman answered, with a touch of irony in his voice, "you go away in some quiet spot and count yourself. When you get done you'll find you aren't so many. You needn't think you're the only boy that can get a job in the mountains."

"Has Toombs captured any game yet?" asked Jimmie.

"I haven't seen him do any hunting," was the answer. "He and Huga just sit around in camp all day and send half-breed messengers scurrying around from place to place."

"So there are half-breed messengers, are there?" demanded Jimmie. "You said there were only two—Toombs and Huga."

"I left New York with Toombs and Huga," answered Norman, "and they're the only ones

I have anything to do with. The half-breeds we found here.''

''All right,'' Jimmie said with a smile, ''we've got Toombs' number right now. If he butts in on us again, we'll roll him down to the foot-hills. What does he want of Ned, anyway?''

''How should I know?'' demanded Norman. ''I'm not his confidential secretary! Say, I'd like to go and live with you boys.''

''Well,'' Jimmie promised, ''you go to Toombs and stay with him until you get Ned out of the mess you got him into, and you can come and live with us, all right.''

The boys sat together under a scraggly pine for a long time, talking about New York and the Wolf Patrol. Norman had joined the Wolves during Jimmie's absence, and so they had not chanced to meet.

''Well,'' Norman said directly, ''I'll have to be getting back to camp. They expect me to build the fire and get the meals.''

''Where is the camp?'' asked Jimmie.

''It's on a shelf not far off,'' was the reply. ''I'm not to tell anybody where it is, but you can find it for yourself if you care to.''

''If I care to?'' repeated Jimmie. ''Don't you suppose I'm going there and help Ned out of the trouble you got him into?''

''Go as far as you like,'' Norman replied,

"only I advise you to keep away from there. Those men are dangerous."

"Then will you help Ned away?"

"I'll do what I can," answered Norman gravely. "I can't tell you, just now, all about the situation I'm in, but you'll probably know sometime that I didn't play crooked."

"I'm going to tag along when you go back to camp!" warned Jimmie.

"Then keep a long ways behind," Norman replied. "When I get to the top of that little elevation over there," he went on, "I'll make the Wolf call again and you come along. Only," he continued, "don't try to get into the camp alone. There's a whole regiment of half-breeds sneaking around. Perhaps some of them have followed me here."

Norman disappeared in the undergrowth, and Jimmie sat waiting for the signal agreed upon. He waited a long time but no signal came.

"Now I wonder," he thought, "if that Boy Scout was acting on the level. I wonder if he won't give me away to that man Toombs and his bunch of half-breeds. I believe he's crooked after all! Think I'll sneak."

He arose from his position by the tree and turned toward the camp. He had proceeded but a short distance, however, when he tripped and fell over a running vine. Before he could regain his feet he was seized by two pair of muscular hands and laid flat on his back. A knife large enough to cut a hole in the side of a house was held to his throat.

"Oh, you, Norman," he said under his breath, "if I just had that scrawny neck of yours in my hands now!"

The boy's rage against the one who had apparently betrayed him was so overpowering that for a moment he paid little attention to the two half-breeds bent over him. Then he saw that the vine over which he had fallen had been purposely held in front of his feet.

His captors were dusky fellows, with straight black, greasy hair and narrow, treacherous black eyes. They seemed to the boy to be crosses between Mexican and California Indians. Directly Jimmie was hustled to his feet by a muscular hand at his collar and his automatic revolver, searchlight and even his pocket knife taken from him.

"Say," Jimmie said, "if I had one of you fellows on the Bowery, somewhere down near Stanton street, I wouldn't do a thing to him."

"You bright boy!" grunted one of the half-breeds as the two started away with their prisoner. "You ver' bright boy!"

They did not take the precaution to bind the boy in any way, but they gave no chance of escape, for every step of the way muscular hands clung to him. The way was rough, for it led directly up the slope, and this mode of surveillance was rather helpful than otherwise in the steep climb.

"Say," Jimmie demanded after a long walk, "did that kid who talked with me tell you to follow him and get me?"

"You one fool boy!" declared one of his captors. "You have your eyes in the wool!"

## CHAPTER VI

### A BRIBE OF HALF A MILLION

Preceded by the boy who had brought the note, Ned walked swiftly along the side of the mountain for a mile or more, taking a northerly course. It is needless to say that the boy was more than suspicious regarding the authenticity of the message he had received.

In the first place, the handwriting on the piece of paper was not at all like that of either of the boys who were alleged to have sent it. In the second place, the boys were never known to carry writing paper with them on their trips out from the camp.

There was a chance, however, that either Jimmie or Frank had written the message at a moment of peril or during great excitement. There was a bare chance, too, that one of them had discovered a sheet of writing paper in his pocket.

The appeal for help, suspicious as it was, was by no means to be disregarded, so Ned trudged along behind his guide, feeling that whatever took place he was doing his full duty.

And there was another feature of the case

which Ned considered fully.  Should the sending of the message prove to be a trick on the part of some designing person, it was quite important that he should know who that person was.  His decision to follow the boy, therefore, was brought about by these two reasons.

It will be remembered that up to the time of Ned's departure from camp, no suspicion of any hostile presence in the mountains had been entertained.  Gilroy, the fat, confidential clerk, it will be remembered, arrived shortly after Ned's departure in response to the message.

Realizing that the messenger might be leading him into a trap, Ned took occasion to blaze his trail by marks on trees, carelessly made, by signs in twigs and by signs in stones.  All these, he knew, would be readily understood by anyone of his chums, or, in fact, by any Boy Scout.

Once or twice Ned thought he caught in the eye of his guide a significant look as these signs were left in the path.  However, the boy made no objections to Ned's frequent pauses, and gave no indications of displeasure at the marking of the trail.

After a long walk along the slope of the mountain toward the north, the boy suddenly turned straight west and made his way up toward the snow line.  Here the walking was very difficult, as the boys were obliged to wind around jutting crags and climb into and out of narrow canyons at the bottoms of which trickles of water made their way eastward.

Up to this time very little conversation had been indulged in, but now during the frequent necessary halts, Ned began questioning his strange companion. The boy answered in a manner which at first seemed entirely frank.

"How did you like the bread and beans?" Ned asked at one resting place with a smile. "Why didn't you wake us up?"

"What are you talking about bread and beans?" asked the boy, though the sly look in his face told Ned that he understood.

"The next time you come to our camp in the night," Ned went on, "just wake us up and we'll give you a night lunch worth while."

"What about last night?" asked the boy.

"Last night," Ned answered, "you would have had broiled bear steak and hot coffee. Steak beats cold beans, doesn't it?"

"Say, you are a good fellow!" exclaimed the guide.

Ned laughingly extended his right hand, giving the full Boy Scout salute. The guide returned the sign and asked:

"How did you know?"

"The button under the lapel of your coat

shows when you are climbing," Ned replied.
"Why do you try to hide it?"

"I put it there so it wouldn't get lost," was
the hesitating answer.

"What time did you reach our camp last
night?" was Ned's next question.

"A little after twelve," was the reply. "It's
a wonder you fellows wouldn't keep some one
on watch. The bears 'll eat you up some
night!"

"Why did you come to the camp at all?"

"Well, I was wandering over the mountains
when you boys came in late yesterday afternoon, and I thought I would go over and have a
visit with you. After I got to your camp I
thought perhaps you wouldn't like to be routed
out of bed, so I just helped myself to a lunch
and came away. Say, but I was good and
hungry!"

"What are you doing in the mountains?"
asked Ned.

"I came in with hunters from New York,"
was the answer.

"So you live in New York city, do you?"

"Yes," was the slow reply.

"And belong to the Wolf Patrol, your button
says!"

"Yes, I belong to the Wolf Patrol."

"Where are you taking me now?" asked Ned, at another stop.

"Why, to the place where the boys are," was the reply.

At that moment Ned understood that the guide was not telling the truth. There was a look in the fellow's eyes which betrayed the fact. However, he decided to continue the journey and discover if possible why the fraudulent message had been sent.

"Who gave you this message?" he finally asked.

"The man who saw the boys," was the answer.

"Then you did not see the boys?"

"Yes," was the slow reply, "I saw the boys."

"Did you speak with them?'

"Yes, I spoke with them," replied the guide.

"Did they give you this note? If so, tell me under what circumstances it was written. It says that they are in need of assistance. Tell me the exact situation of affairs."

Instead of replying to the direct question, the guide darted away, passing around a corner of rock, and was soon lost to view. Ned hesitated, not knowing whether he ought to follow him or not.

While he stood considering the matter, four as evil-looking half-breeds as he had ever seen swarmed down upon him, and in a moment he was bound hand and foot and placed on a rude stretcher.

The attack had come so suddenly that the boy had offered little resistance. He now lay upon the stretcher of bark and boughs and looked into the faces of his captors with curiosity as well as astonishment.

"What did you do that for?" he asked.

The individual who seemed to be the leader of the party mumbled out some sullen reply and motioned to the others to take up the litter.

"Anyway," the boy said grimly, "I seem to be going in state."

"You are a slippery cuss!" the leader declared and the little procession moved on up the slope.

All four of the men seemed to be half-breeds, dirty and roughly clad. Ned felt a feeling of repulsion which would have been expressed by blows had his feet and hands been at liberty.

The climb up the mountain was a slow one, and one not at all pleasant to the boy as they insisted on carrying him feet foremost. At last, however, they came to a level shelf of fair size whereon a tent had been pitched.

There was a fire in front of the tent, and a large, fleshy, well-dressed man sat on a packing box industriously whittling a pine stick. Not far away, and bent over a mass of dirty dishes, was a man who seemed to be older and a great deal taller than the man on the box.

This latter individual's face was thin and dark and lighted by a pair of eyes which seemed almost lidless, like those of a snake. Both men were very neatly dressed in tailor-made garments although the articles of clothing showed the effects of mountain climbing.

The litter was set down in front of the tent and Ned lost no time in taking a sitting position. The fat man looked him over benevolently.

"Well, son," he said in a moment, "you made no effort to make my acquaintance, and so I sent the boys to ask you over."

"They did it all right!" Ned answered.

The fat man now motioned to the half-breeds, who proceeded to search the boy for weapons and then cut his bonds.

"Now," said the fat man, "we may as well introduce ourselves. You are Ned Nestor, I take it? Well, my name is Richard Toombs, recently of the city of New York."

"How did you happen to escape?" asked Ned scornfully.

"Now don't make the mistake of becoming sarcastic!" Toombs warned. "I had you brought here because I can do you a service and you can do me one. We'll get along all right together if you exercise the good sense you are generally given credit for possessing."

"If you wanted to see me," Ned demanded angrily, "why didn't you come over to the camp? Why did you send your cut-throats over to tie me up like a pig for roasting?"

"Because," Toombs answered, "you have the reputation in New York of being a very obstinate as well as a very clever lad. Because, again," he went on, "I have no time to waste in preliminaries. I wanted you to understand from the word 'Go' just exactly what the situation is."

"Well, what is it?" asked Ned.

"You came into the mountains with young Jack Bosworth?"

"Jack is a member of my party," Ned answered.

"And you came on a mission for Jack's father?"

"Nothing of the kind!" answered Ned. "We came in on a vacation."

"You don't expect me to believe that, do you?" demanded Toombs.

"It is the truth," answered Ned.

"It is remarkable," smiled Toombs, "that Jack Bosworth's son and you, a juvenile detective of pronounced ability, should just happen into this country at this particular time!"

"What do you think we came in for?" asked Ned.

"Young man," Toombs answered, "a good many million dollars depend upon the finding of certain records. I, representing various claimants, am informed that Jack Bosworth, Senior, the scheming corporation lawyer, has definite information concerning the whereabouts of those papers. It is my belief that you came here to seize and destroy them."

"Well," Ned said with a smile, "if you believe that, you certainly have acted unwisely. It strikes me that the correct thing for you to have done was to have waited until I secured the papers before you declared yourself my enemy. Can't you see that?"

"No, I can't!" was the reply. "The papers would not last five minutes after coming into your hands."

"I tell you," Ned replied lightly, "I don't know anything about the papers of which you speak. We came here on a vacation, and that is all there is to it. You have made a mistake, and my advice to you is to rectify it at the earliest possible moment."

"Well," Toombs said, "if you insist on sticking to a lie like that, I can't help it. I'll give you fair warning, however, that you must consider yourself my guest until I get an entirely different answer from you. I hope we'll get along well together. You'll be well treated."

Ned turned his eyes away from the broad, fat, smooth face of Toombs to catch a glimpse of the boy messenger standing at a corner of the tent. It seemed to Ned for an instant that the boy was about to communicate with him by sign or word. Then his face changed into one of sullen defiance and he passed from view.

"Who is that boy?" asked Ned. "The messenger who brought the note, I mean? Did he write the note himself?"

"No," answered Toombs, "I wrote the note. We were together—the boy and I—on the slope below your camp, and he caught sight of two of your chums. Then it occurred to me to send for you in the name of the boys. He only delivered the note—I wrote it."

"It's a wonder you didn't send your half-breeds out after the boys, too," Ned said. "You might have lugged them away easily enough, I presume."

"Now, see here," Toombs went on, "I don't want any trouble with your friends or with you. I'll make you a fair business proposition. Tell me the plans of this tricky corporation lawyer you are serving; tell me where to find the papers you came here in trace of, and I'll give you half a million dollars. Now," the fat man went on, "perhaps you will understand why I did not molest any of your chums and why no harm came to any of you when my men were at your camp at midnight."

"And if I refuse to accept this monstrous bribe?" Ned asked.

"Then no one will ever know that the offer was made or refused," declared Toombs with an evil gleam in his eyes.

## CHAPTER VII

### THE FRANCISCAN MISSION

"Now, I wonder," Jimmie mused as he was forced along by the two half-breeds, "whether I won't get a chance before long to show these ginks how fast I can run. I sure could do something of a stunt on my feet if I had an opportunity right now."

During one of the brief breathing spells, when the half-breeds paused for an instant on a level ledge of rock, the boy turned to the east and faced the pines in the vicinity of which he had been captured. In the distance he could see the granite finger sticking up like a mile-post in the green of the trees.

"Judging from the course we have taken, and the distance we have traveled," the boy mused, "we ought to be somewhere in the vicinity of the parallelogram I saw in the snow. Only," he added ruefully, "it's quite a climb up to that point yet."

He was thinking of the story Gilroy had told of the ruined mission; of the walls in ruins, and the subterranean rooms and passages farther back in the heart of the hill.

"'It would just be my luck," he mused grimly, "'to discover that ruined mission, and lead the way into the basement of that old peak. If I get a chance to break away from these half-breeds, I'll make a run in that direction anyway."

From that time on the boy pretended great fatigue. He insisted on frequent rests, and always lay down panting whenever his captors halted in their clumsy ascent of the slope. The half-breeds regarded the boy with scornful glances at such times, as if expressing contempt for one unable to endure an ordinary journey up a mountainside.

The boy was perfectly willing that they should believe him to be exhausted by his efforts. When, after a few short rests, they dropped their hands away from his arms, he experienced a thrill of hope.

At last his opportunity came. The half-breeds became less watchful as time passed on. They even turned their snaky eyes away from him at times, looking over the valley below and conversing together in a language he could not understand.

Watching his opportunity, when their eyes were directed in another direction, the boy sprang away and ran as nimbly as a mountain goat up the acclivity. The half-breeds were so astonished at the sudden action of the boy; so utterly bewildered by the speed he made, that for a moment they made no effort to stop him.

When at last they sprang after him, threatening to shoot if he did not halt instantly, it was too late. Jimmie passed around a ledge of rock and was soon out of their sight.

The remainder of that race for freedom always came back to the boy's mind as a bit of nightmare. He ran swiftly along ledges, bounded over boulders, dipped breathlessly into gulches, and clung to precipitous sides with his bare fingers until it seemed that he must drop from sheer exhaustion. At last he came to a canyon wider and deeper than any which he had yet encountered.

He scrambled down the slope, always pursued by fragments of rocks from above, and presently landed a hundred feet below on a shelf which seemed to promise temporary safety. Panting and trembling from the exertion, came in every limb, he listened for sounds of pursuit but none came to his ears.

Sitting on the narrow ledge, his back against and almost vertical wall, he realized that he had climbed to a great distance, for he shivered in his warm clothing and the sharp sting of frosty air was in his nostrils. Without knowing it, he had actually entered the region of snow.

After a time composure came back with his breath, and he began looking around in the hope of finding some way out which did not lead in the direction his pursuers were probably taking. Then his attention was attracted to the shelf upon which he sat.

It seemed to him that at some time in the distant past crude steps had been cut in the ledge and along the wall leading into the gorge below. Melting snows and the storms of many winters had, in a measure, obliterated the sharp outlines of the treads, but still the boy saw the work of man in the arrangement.

After a time he arose lamely to his feet and walked along in the direction pointed out by the crude stairway. Directly he came to an opening in the wall of the precipice.

Realizing that the cave would at least serve as a hiding place, the boy entered and looked about. The place was dark and damp. A flock of bats, stirred into activity by his approach, flew in his face and winged their way toward the brilliant sunshine beyond.

Jimmie would have given a good deal just at that time for one of the dozen or more searchlights which lay at the camp. There was no knowing how far the passage extended into the mountain, and it was very dark.

For all he knew it might be intersected by

passages worn away by subterranean streams. Presently he remembered that a good supply of matches which he had acquired that morning had not been taken away from him. Lighting one, he saw that the floor of the passage was remarkably smooth and free from obstructions. The walls were also smooth, and held, here and there, shallow openings which seemed to have been artificially produced. As he proceeded through the tunnel-like place he became aware of a damp chill wind blowing directly upon him.

As the passage narrowed, the current of air became stronger, and before long the boy found it impossible to use matches without wasting them. Presently he found that by extending his arms he could touch the walls on either side. The stones were, of course, damp and loathesome to the touch.

Only for a remarkable discovery made through the medium of his fingers, he might then have abandoned further investigation of the grewsome place. His discovery was this:

The passage through which he was moving was of artificial construction!

The walls showed traces of rude chisel work!

After a time the walls drew back so that he was unable to reach them even by taking a few steps to right and left. It seemed, too, that he had passed out of the current of air.

"Its dollars to rotten apples," mused the boy, exultant though anxious, "that I have blundered into some old-time robber den, or into the subterranean rooms of the old Franciscan mission."

The thought was exhilarating, and the boy notwithstanding the peril in which he believed himself to be, danced gaily about for a moment. As he did so, one foot slipped over the edge of a declivity and he went rolling down, down, in the darkness to a lower level.

"Whoever built this idiotic contraption," the boy declared, feeling of his arms and legs to see if they were still whole, "neglected to put in elevators, but I found a way to get down stairs, all the same!"

While the boy sat on the rocky floor rubbing the bruised knee upon which he had fallen, a ray of light shone upon a wall directly in front of him. He turned quickly about and saw the round eye of a searchlight fixed upon the ceiling.

He crouched closer to the floor and waited. It seemed to him that the person in charge of the light must have seen him. Still he hoped that such was not the case. The light advanced nearer to where he sat and so he crawled stealthily away.

"I am a child of fortune, sure enough!" chuckled the boy after the immediate danger of discovery had passed. "First thing I know, I'll find a banquet room in here with a table loaded down with haunches of venison and great tankards of nut-brown ale."

While the boy crouched in the corner the light passed him and turned into a passage leading to the east. Then he heard the sound of voices—low, fierce voices, speaking in English.

"And you let him escape!" one said.

"I tell you he rose up in the air and flew like a bird!" another voice exclaimed. "No living person ever saw such an exhibition before!"

"But still, you let him escape!" the first speaker repeated.

"He only got away!" was the answer. "He is somewhere in this vicinity and we'll get him before nightfall."

"As well look for a diamond in the bottom of the Atlantic!" snarled the other. "I have sent the men out in the search, but have no hope of their getting hold of him."

"That's me!" mused Jimmie. "That's me they're talking about trying to get hold of."

"Well, we may as well go back to camp," said the first speaker. "There is no profit in arguing here."

Jimmie crept forward toward the light and saw a large, fat, smooth-faced man and a tall man with a thin face standing in a narrow chamber which seemed to have been fairly well furnished once, but which now held only decaying tables, chairs and couches. It was the tall, dark man who held the light. As Jimmie looked, he laid it down on a tottering table to make and light a cigarette.

His mind busy with a daring thought, Jimmie crept into the chamber and watched for the opportunity he sought. The men were talking together in lower tones now, and seemed to be very much interested in the subject under discussion. As they spoke, they both walked excitedly up and down the little chamber, brushing against the decaying articles of furniture whenever they by chance left the pathway shown by the light.

Jimmie advanced toward the table and finally succeeded in crawling under it. Then, waiting until they were at the farther end of their promenade, at the extreme distance from the lamp, he reached cautiously out and switched off the light.

In the darkness which followed he gave the table a slight push and sent it clattering to the floor and, with the light in his possession, darted out in the direction of the passage by which he had entered.

''Now, we'll have a job finding that electric!''

one of the men said angrily. "Light a match, will you?"

"I have just used my last match," was the discouraging reply.

"Well, I never carry matches," the first speaker said, "but we ought to be able to find the electric easily enough in the darkness."

"Strange what made it go out," one said.

"Didn't you hear the table fall?" demanded the other.

"I remember now," was the answer. "The lamp is probably broken, so we may as well find our way out without looking for it."

"You have my permission to do that," chuckled Jimmie from his now secure hiding place.

The two men stumbled about in the darkness for a minute, and the boy knew that they were feeling their way to some entrance other than the one by which he had found his way into the cave. Before long their footsteps and their voices died away, and then he advanced into the little chamber where they had stood.

"The old mission, all right!" he thought.

While he looked around other footsteps were heard, followed by the sound of a struggle.

"Hold fast!" some one shouted.

"Hold fast yourself!" was the smothered

reply. "What do you mean by letting go of the fellow in that way?"

"I didn't let go. I've got hold of him yet!"

"Oh, you fool!" shouted the other. "That's my arm you've got hold of! Where's your light?"

"I dropped it in the fight," was the answer. "Go on away and get one. He's somewhere in the cave, and its a sure thing he can't get out. Tell the boys to guard all the entrances. That fool of a Toombs did a smart thing when he told us we needn't keep him tied!"

Jimmie heard running footsteps for an instant and then came silence.

"Now I wonder," he thought, "if they've gone and captured some of the boys and brought them here. They may have the whole bunch by this time for all I know. I wonder if I dare turn on this light."

Instead of doing so, however, he sat perfectly still and listened to a soft tread approaching the spot where he stood. Whoever the visitor was, he was short of breath for he came along panting as if winded by a long struggle.

"I'll take a chance on the light," he mused.

And the next instant the room was illuminated.

## CHAPTER VIII

### A QUEER HIDING PLACE

When Jimmie turned on the searchlight in the cavern, he half expected to see the hostile face of one of the half-breeds. Instead, the light revealed Ned, standing in an attitude of defense, a stone of good size balanced in each hand. The light went out instantly.

The situation was now doubly alarming, it being well-known to the outlaws that Ned was at liberty somewhere within the cavern. It was certain that they would soon enter the place in full force, with plenty of light, in which case it seemed that both boys would surely be discovered.

Still, so great was the joy of the boys at the unexpected meeting, that, in spite of the general peril of the situation, they seized each other like baby bears and danced madly about.

"Where did you come from, Jimmie?" demanded Ned, still breathless.

"Oh, I was invited to this part of the country," the boy replied, "and came in here by accident. And so, then," he continued, "that message was a fake one after all!"

"Yes, it was a fake message, of course, because you boys never sent it," laughed Ned, "but we mustn't stop here to explain matters," he continued. "Those fellows will be in here thicker than bees around honey in a short time, and we must find some way of eluding them."

"I know the way out!" Jimmie answered. "There's a long passage leading to a gorge on the side of the mountain, and if we can get up to that, we can slip away without any one knowing anything about it."

"I'm afraid the outlaws know and are guarding all the entrances," Ned answered.

"Well, if they know this one, they don't use it," Jimmie insisted, "because the elevator isn't working, and there isn't any staircase, and I came near breaking my neck tumbling down a chute from the passage into the next room. I believe we can make a sneak that way!"

"We may as well try," Ned agreed, "for we can gain nothing by remaining inactive. Turn on your light, and we'll make a break for the place where you got your tumble."

"Is it safe to turn on the light?" asked Jimmie.

"It is safer now than it will be in a few minutes," Ned answered.

"What's the answer to that?" demanded Jimmie.

"Why, the outlaws are doubtless collecting their forces now, and in a very short time they'll be rummaging every nook and corner of this hole in the ground.  We certainly can't show a light after they get in here."

"I should have known that!" Jimmie exclaimed.  "I think I'm getting pretty dense, anyhow.  Say, Ned," the boy went on, "is it absolutely necessary for us to get captured, and tied up, and imprisoned, and shut up in some old hole, every time we go out on a vacation trip?"

"You can't go out looking for adventures and have things come your way all the time," suggested Ned.  "Now, turn on your light," he continued, "and we'll make a quick break for the passage by which you entered.  The minute you see the passage, turn out your light and we'll find our way in the dark."

"I'm afraid we'll need wings to get up into the passage," Jimmie suggested.  "It seems to me that I fell far enough to hit the pavement from the top of Madison Square Garden."

"Well, get to going!" urged Ned.  "Get a move on!  For all we know they may be lurking around here now."

Jimmie switched on the light, whirled it over the dilapidated and rotting furniture for an instant, then shot into the next chamber, and from

that into a by-passage by way of which he had
entered. The floor of this by-passage stood at
an angle of about fifty degrees, and the boys
were preparing to undertake the climb when
shouts came from the rear, and a great light
filled the room they had just left.

"We can never get up there now!" Ned
whispered. "We've got to take a run for it!"

"Huh!" returned Jimmie, "we can run only
around in a circle, and there's enough of them
to wear us out in a few minutes. What we've
got to do right now is to find a hiding place!"

At great risk of discovery, Ned seized the
flashlight and pressed the spring. The illumination showed a moldy chamber with
water dripping from the walls in places.

At some distant day the chamber had evidently been occupied by human beings, for a
great fire-place was cut in the rock at one end,
and there were niches in the wall which had
doubtless been used for storage. The floor was
smooth, showing the work of human hands.

"Get onto the fire-place!" whispered Jimmie.
'Where do you suppose the smoke goes?
There's no chimney on the mountain."

"Probably it escapes through some opening
in the rock," Ned answered.

"Do you suppose," Jimmie asked, "that the
smoke vent is large enough for us to hide in?"

Before the words were out of the boy's mouth, Ned was making toward the fireplace. The light was out now, but Jimmie had no difficulty in following the boy in the darkness.

"Ned!" he called softly in a moment.

"Come on up!" whispered Ned.

"Turn on the light, then," Jimmie advised.

Ned switched on the electric, but kept it inside the chimney into which he had climbed. Only a faint radiance reached the opening below.

"Give me your hand," whispered Ned, "and I'll give you a lift."

The sound of voices and footsteps now echoed loudly through the cavern. Lights were flashing here and there, and when Jimmie at last found himself inside the chimney, he knew that the very room he had recently left was being occupied by the outlaws.

The electric light was out again, and the boy groped with his hands in the darkness. Much to his surprise they failed to locate his chum.

"Ned!" he called softly. "Where are you hiding?"

Jimmie heard a chuckle in the darkness and felt a hand on his shoulder. Then Ned whispered in his ear:

"I guess I've stumbled on one of the hidden cells of the mission!" he said. "Anyway there's a hole leading out of this chimney that's big enough to keep house in."

"We'll be finding a train of cars and an East river ferryboat next," Jimmie chuckled. "We always do find something when we go away from camp. If we don't find anything else, we find trouble."

It was thought safe, now, to turn on the electric light. The rays showed a room perhaps twelve feet in size with furniture and furnishings of the description of those in the chamber below. Although the apartment seemed to be somewhere near the center of a lofty finger of rock which lifted from the eastern slope of the mountain, the air was remarkably fresh and pure.

"There's an opening somewhere," Ned suggested. "A shut-in room like this would asphyxiate one if there were no ventilation."

"Then I think we'd better be finding it!" Jimmie advised. "Just listen to those fellows chewing the rag in the room we recently left!"

The boys remained perfectly silent, then, and listened. There seemed to be several men in the chamber below, and two were talking in angry tones. There were plenty of torches below, too, for the red flare and the stink of them came into the boys' hiding place by way of the fire-niche below. This is what the boys heard:

"You can see for yourself, Huga," a voice which Ned recognized as that of Toombs, was saying, "that the boy is not here."

"But I am certain I heard footsteps running in this direction when I stood in the darkness before you men came in!" Huga answered. "He must be in this chamber somewhere."

"Look for yourself!" Toombs advised crossly.

"Isn't there some hiding place in the walls?" asked Huga.

Ned nudged Jimmie as they heard this, and both moved farther back in the hiding place. It will be understood how intently they listened for the next sentence.

"You ought to know that," Toombs answered; "you are supposed to know all about this old mission, while I am fresh from Wall street."

"I have never heard of any secret passage or room in this part of the excavation," the half-breed replied.

"Then stop arguing that the boy is here!" roared Toombs.

Huga made no reply, but the boys heard him poking about in the fireplace. Presently a light flashed into the chimney.

"He's after us now all right!" whispered Jimmie.

"Keep still, you little dunce!" Ned said.

"If he sticks his head up here, soak him!" advised Jimmie.

"Don't you think I won't," Ned returned.

But Huga did not enter the huge old fireplace at all. When he flashed his light into the chimney he saw only straight up, and the vertical passage from the fire-flue was too small for even a small cat to negotiate.

The chamber into which the boys had found their way was directly at the back of the flue, and might have been seen by a more careful man. The boys chuckled as the half-breed turned away.

In a few minutes the sounds of pursuit ceased entirely. Lights no longer flashed about the room, creating a faint mist in the fireplace below. Still the boys were not certain that the outlaws had abandoned the hunt.

"Say, Ned," Jimmie whispered, directly, poking Ned in the ribs, "you didn't bring one of those bear steaks with you, did you?"

"Why, Jimmie," Ned said in pretended amazement, "you're not getting hungry, are you? I'm astonished at that!"

"Hungry!" repeated the boy. "I feel as if I could eat my way through this rock like a mouse eats through cheese! And I could drink a barrel of water. There never was such a thirst."

"Well," Ned suggested, "we'd better wait here a little while, until things get quieted down, and then make a break for the passage."

"All right," Jimmie said with an air of resignation, "I'll crawl back here in the corner and try to imagine that I'm in charge of a pie wagon on Third avenue. Perhaps I can dream a pie or two!"

The boy leaned back in an angle of the chamber and prepared to continue the discussion regarding the different kinds of pies sold at the old Williams street corner. As he did so, the support of his back gave way, his heels flew up in the air, and he tumbled all of a heap into a passage which seemed to begin at that corner of the room.

Hearing the fall and the exclamation of impatience which came from the boy's lips, Ned turned on the electric and saw Jimmie lying on his back in a tunnel probably a yard in size each way. There were plenty of indications that the tunnel had been cut through solid rock.

As far as Ned could see; that is, as far as the eye of the electric carried; there were no breaks in it. Directly a chill breeze blew in from the opening, and the boy knew that the passage touched the surface of the mountain not far away.

"Je-rusalem!" shouted Jimmie, "hold up

the light and let me see if I'm all here. That's the second tumble I've got in this consarned old hole today."

"If every tumble you get in life brings such results as this," Ned declared, "you ought to go around the world looking for tumbles!"

"They hurt, just the same!" Jimmie declared, rubbing the back of his head. "I got an awful bump on my coco!"

"Well, crowd along!" advised Ned.

"Crowd along?" repeated Jimmie. "What for?"

"Use your nose," advised Ned.

Jimmie sniffed elaborately and hit Ned a resounding whack on the back. Then he sat down on the bottom of the passage.

"Say, Ned, look here!" he said. "When we got into this scrape, we didn't look for any old Franciscan monks to help us out, did we? Two or three hundred years ago, when they dug this passage through the rock, they hadn't any idea they were digging it for us, had they?"

"This is a mysterious world," Ned answered. "It seems to be unnecessary for us to plan any mode of escape. The wise old chap who formed the Franciscan order in Europe, hundreds of years ago, prepared the way of escape for us!"

"That's what he did!" answered Jimmie.

"And I wish he had gone a little farther and prepared a good fat meat pie for us."

"Jimmie," Ned chuckled, "some day you'll get into a corner where you won't get anything to eat for a week. I never knew a boy who thought so much of his stomach as you do!"

"May the day be long delayed!" laughed Jimmie.

"Well, crawl along!" Ned advised, "and I'll see if I can get this slab of stone you pushed out back in its place."

It was by no means a difficult task to replace the stone, as it was thin and had been nicely fitted into the opening. In a short time the boys, proceeding mostly on their hands and knees, came to the end of the tunnel and looked out over a valley tucked in between two great summits.

The snow-line was not far away and the air was cold, notwithstanding the direct rays of the sun.

There was no one in sight, no moving object anywhere, as the boys paused at the mouth of the passage and gazed about. Judging from the location of the sun, they were looking straight west.

"Now," Ned said after a pause, "if we follow this little valley straight to the south, we'll come out somewhere near our camp."

"Yes," Jimmie answered, "I have a pious notion that our brownstone front is carved into the face of a continuation of that ridge on the other side of the little valley."

"Perhaps we'll find the Boy Scout messenger at the camp," Ned suggested.

"If we do," Jimmie declared, "I'll change his face for him!"

"I can't understand the fellow," Ned admitted.

"Gee!" cried Jimmie, "He came out into the woods and told Frank and I to beat it, then went up into the camp and led you into the clutches of these outlaws. If I had his head in chancery right now, I'd 'beat it', all right! He ought to get a thousand years!"

"I hope the boys are all safe," said Ned.

Jimmie told his chum of the arrival of Gilroy, and then the two boys hastened toward the camp.

"The outlaws were discussing the advisability of taking all the boys into their care," Ned said, as they hustled along, "so I'm afraid they've been there and taken the lads by surprise."

## CHAPTER IX

### IN QUEST OF INFORMATION

Left at the camp by the departure of Ned and Jimmie, Jack, Frank and Harry sat for a long time in the warm sunshine in front of the barrier and discussed the situation. Gilroy had tucked himself into a collection of blankets at the rear of the cave and was sound asleep.

"What do you think Jimmie had in his mind when he went away alone?" asked Harry. "He merely had some plan to carry out."

"Oh, he's always going off alone," Jack answered.

"Some day he'll go away alone and won't be able to get back!" Frank put in. "He won't always be able to get out of his scrapes."

"Pretty foxy boy, that!" Jack declared.

"What strikes me as being singular," Frank suggested, "is that Jack's father never said a word to him about this land business."

"Father never talks his business over with any one," Jack broke in.

"If we had only known about the outlaws being here in the hills," Harry suggested, "we might have kept out of sight of them for a long time. But, you see, they found us first.''

''And they used a nice, crooked little spy to do it with!'' Frank exclaimed. ''This little alleged Boy Scout who stole our provisions last night, and crept into the woods to tell Jimmie and I to beat it, and then brought a note to Ned to get him away from the camp, must be playing a leading part for the sneaks.''

''He's doing all of that!'' Jack agreed. ''I don't believe he's a Boy Scout at all. He's just picked up a word or two and a sign.''

''Perhaps we'll run across him again,'' Frank said. ''If we do, I'll find out whether he's a Boy Scout or not!''

''Well,'' Jack exclaimed, springing to his feet, ''are we going to sit here all day and let Jimmie do all the hunting? We ought to get out in the mountains and help find Ned.''

''Look here, boys!'' Harry cried, ''do you see anything to the east there that looks at all familiar?''

''Do you mean the smoke coming up over the tops of the trees?'' asked Frank. ''I noticed that several minutes ago.''

''Well, just keep your eye on it,'' Harry advised, ''and see if it brings anything to your mind.''

''Sure it does!'' shouted Frank, all excitement

now. "There are two columns of smoke close together, and you ought to know what that means."

"Indian sign! Boy Scout sign! Means 'Help is wanted'!" exclaimed Harry. "We've got to go and see what it is."

"It may be Jimmie," Jack suggested.

"Its either Jimmie or that messenger boy," Frank said. "If its Jimmie, he's really in trouble, and if its the messenger boy, he's doing it to get more of us into his clutches."

"Then we'd better go well armed and ready for any kind of a reception," Jack advised. "No knowing what we'll find."

"What'll we do with Gilroy?" asked Frank.

"Aw, let him sleep," advised Harry.

"Sure, let him sleep," Jack put in. "He'll be all right 'till we get back. No one will molest the camp in daytime."

"Seems to me that we ought to leave someone here," Frank said.

"All right, you can stay if you want to!" Jack declared. "Harry and I are going down there to see what the trouble is about."

"Aw, come on, Frank!" Harry urged. "There won't anything happen to Gilroy! He may have a bad dream, but that's about all."

"How far do you suppose that signal is from here?" asked Frank.

"Not more than half a mile," Harry explained.

"Then I'll go," Frank decided. "I don't like the idea of sitting around the camp and letting you boys have all the fun. Besides," he continued, "if it is the messenger who is making the signals, you'll need all the help you can get."

"Come running, then!" advised Jack, starting down the slope.

As the reader will remember, the signal observed by the boys had been built by Jimmie in the hope of attracting the attention of Ned, or of Norman, the boy who had made himself so conspicuous that morning. In building the fires and creating the columns of dense white smoke by heaping on green boughs, the boy had not given serious thought to the effect his action might have on his chums.

In fact, at the time of his leaving camp, he had not fully decided what course to pursue, and for this reason he had not informed the boys of his intention to set a signal for the benefit of the mysterious Boy Scout. Even at the time of making the signal, he had no idea that it would actually draw his three chums away from the camp.

He might have known what the effect would be, but, though he did stop to consider for a moment, he did not take in the whole situation.

Jimmie usually acted on impulse, and so the signal lifted to the sky without any explanation having been made to the Boy Scouts who were certain to see it.

It will be remembered that when Jimmie descended from the elevation where the fires had been built he did so in order to hasten in the direction of a smoke signal which he saw to the north. The result of this was that he was out of the vicinity of the fires long before the boys reached that point.

When the three lads came to the finger of granite upon the top of which the two fires showed, they first made a careful examination of the thickets close by and then ascended to the top.

"These fires were made to constitute a signal, all right!" Jack declared, poking at the now dying embers.

"Sure!" answered Frank. "You see, no cooking was done here, and there is no camp in sight."

"Besides, the position of the blazes on this high rock shows that the fires were built so that the columns of smoke might be seen," suggested Harry. "It was Indian talk, all right!"

"Well, there's no one here in need of help so far as I can see!" laughed Jack, "and so we may as well go back to the camp."

"That's the thing to do," Frank urged. "To tell the truth, I don't feel exactly right about leaving Gilroy there alone."

"Aw, we'll hear him sleeping before we get within a rod of the cave," laughed Jack. "Gilroy is a good old chap, and father thinks a lot of him, but he doesn't know much about this kind of a life. I'll bet that right now he's dreaming about grizzly bears, and lions, and crocodiles, and panthers."

From their position in the forest, after their departure from the rock, they could see nothing of the signal from the north which had attracted Jimmie's attention, so there seemed nothing for them to do but to return to camp. Therefore they set out at good speed.

After a short walk, Jack beckoned the boys to his side and suggested that they take a route to the camp different from that which they had followed on leaving it.

"You see, boys," he explained, "that was a signal, all right, and we haven't found out the cause of it. So far as we know, it was put up to get us away from the camp."

"I'm beginning to think it was," Frank announced. "Either to get us away from the camp for the purpose of capturing us, or for the purpose of raiding our provisions."

"Well," Jack went on, "if we duck away to

the south and return to the camp by a new course, anyone watching for us might watch in vain."

"That's the idea!" Harry answered.

"Then here we go the south," Frank suggested, starting away at as swift a gait as was possible in the thicket.

They had proceeded but a short distance when every tree bole of good size immediately in front of them seemed to their astonished eyes to yield a scowling, dirty half-breed. The boys drew their guns.

"No use, lads!" a voice said, speaking in good English. "The men in the bushes have you covered. Anyway, there's no harm intended."

"Why the holdup?" demanded Jack.

The man who had spoken now advanced to Jack and looked him keenly in the face. Although carrying the general appearance of the gang of half-breeds at his back, the boys could see by the fellow's face and manner that he was different from the others.

"You are Jack Bosworth?" he asked.

"That's my name," replied the boy.

"You are here on a mission for your father?"

"I am here on a hunting trip."

"With business on the side, eh?"

"No business at all," replied Jack.

"We know better than that!" the stranger answered.

"What do you want of us?" asked Jack.

"We want information now in your possession," answered the fellow, looking Jack sharply in the eyes.

"What kind of information?"

"We want to know where certain documents are."

"You'll have to ask some one else, then."

"We are certain that you have the information we require."

"If I had," Jack answered, "you never would get it from me."

"You will gain nothing by being obstinate," the fellow said.   "Remember that we have Ned Nestor, the alleged juvenile detective, at our camp.   He seems inclined to keep what information he possesses to himself, and, before proceeding to extreme measures with him, we decided to lay the case before you.   I am afraid Nestor will receive rough treatment at the hands of my allies unless the information they demand is given them."

"So that was a lying message you sent Nestor, was it?"

"There's no use in discussing the matter at length," the other stated.   "I think I'd better take you boys into camp and let the boss talk

with you.   And let me warn you now, before
anything more is said, not to attempt resistance.
If you do, there'll be shooting done, and it won't
be my men who will get hurt!   Now, face about
to the north and march away to camp, like good
little boys.   We don't want to hurt you, but we
insist on having our way in the matter of this
information.   Perhaps Nestor may be able to
convince you that you ought not to be so
obstinate."

"I don't think Nestor will attempt anything
of the kind," replied Jack, "and I think that
you are a great big bluff!"

## CHAPTER X

### GILROY AND THE BEAR

When, at last, Ned and Jimmie, still watching about for hostile forces, came to the barricaded camp, the fire had burned down and no one was in sight. Ned regarded the wall of rock with a smile.

"Isn't that great?" Jimmie asked.

"I'm afraid it wouldn't do much good in case of an attack," Ned suggested. "We'd soon get hungry and thirsty and have to surrender."

"Anyway, its an all right thing to shoot from!" Jimmie announced. "If you'd seen the way we sweat rolling those rocks, you'd think it was all right, anyway. I wonder where the boys are."

"I was thinking more about the boys than about the barricade," Ned admitted. "Were they all here when you left?"

"All sitting in front of the entrance," Jimmie replied, "except Gilroy, and he was asleep on a pile of blankets in the cave."

"He may be there yet," suggested Ned. "Suppose we go and see."

Jimmie made his way through the narrow

entrance, found a searchlight, and turned a round circle of flame on a great heap of blankets in a back corner.   There was no one in the cave at all save only himself.

Before returning to report to Ned, the hungry boy seized a plate of corn pones and a can of tinned beans from the provision chest.

"Look here, Ned," he said in a moment, appearing before his chum with his mouth full of beans, "the appetite of our midnight visitor seems to be for confidential clerks as well as for bread.  Someone has stolen Gilroy!  Anyway, he's not in the cave!"

"He may have gone away with the boys," suggested Ned.

"He wasn't thinking of going away with the boys when I left," Jimmie answered.  "He was telling how much he liked New York, and how he'd like to pound his ear for about three days and nights."

"Anyway," Ned decided, "we'll wait here a little while and see if they don't return.   In the meantime, you can get yourself something to eat."

"Don't you call this something to eat?" asked Jimmie.

"One poor little can of beans and one poor little plate of corn pones won't make much of an impression on your appetite," Ned laughed.

"What you need is one of those neat little bear steaks, about as large as a warming pan. You'll have plenty of time in which to cook it."

"And that means that I can cook one for you, too?" asked Jimmie.

"Why, of course you can!" returned Ned.

"I'd like to cook one for the Boy Scout who got us both into such trouble," Jimmie declared. "I'd put poison on it!"

"Now, don't you be too severe on that Boy Scout," Ned advised. "According to your own story, he warned you and Frank in the thicket, and I know very well that he wanted to tell me something, but didn't dare do it."

"Well, here's another thing," Jimmie explained. "When I went out to look for you, I gave the 'help' smoke signal from the top of a granite rock in the pines. In five minutes after the columns of smoke became large enough to be seen at a distance, the signal was answered from the north, it seemed to me from the vicinity of the old mission. Now, of course, you didn't send out that signal."

"I rather think not," smiled Ned.

"Then it was sent up by this crooked messenger boy with the intention of getting us out to look for you. He believed, of course, that we would regard the call for help as coming from you and rush away from camp."

"Don't be too sure of that," warned Ned. "There's something about that boy I rather like. Besides, he really is a member of the Wolf Patrol, New York."

"My own patrol?" exclaimed Jimmie. "I never saw him at the club room. He told me that he belonged to the Wolf Patrol, but I didn't believe it. I think he's a fake."

"Time alone will tell," answered Ned. "I'm going to believe in the boy until I get some positive proof that he really is crooked."

Jimmie was about to continue the argument when a succession of shrieks and calls for help came from the forest on the slope below.

"Now, what's that?" demanded Jimmie. "That isn't any of our boys!"

"Help! Help! Help!" cried the voice.

"No," Ned agreed, "our boys don't make a racket like that."

"Say!" Jimmie shouted, springing to his feet. "I bet you the next dollar I don't find that that's the fat clerk, Gilroy!"

"The voice sounds like that of a fat man," Ned laughed.

"Gilroy's fat all right!" Jimmie exclaimed. "He's got one of those pink baby faces that make you hungry to look at. He makes me think of a roast of veal, and he's got a cute little round bald spot on the top of his head.

And he wants to be dignified and speaks his words impressively. Say, Ned," the boy continued, ''I wouldn't mind having that fellow get into some kind of a mixup out here!"

''Oh Lord! Oh Lord! Oh Lord!" cried the voice from the forest.

''That's Gilroy, all right enough!" Ned declared. ''Why don't you go down and see what he wants, Jimmie?" he added.

''Aw, he ain't talking to me!" cried the boy.

''Then I presume I'll have to go," Ned said, rising from his seat in front of the barrier. ''Perhaps he's been stung by a bee."

''He didn't get crippled in his shrieker," Jimmie suggested.

Ned stepped into the cave and secured an automatic revolver to replace the one taken from him at the old mission, and also passed one to Jimmie. Then the two hastened into the forest in the direction of the sounds.

The call for help continued to come, although the voice of the man came hoarser at every call. When the boys finally came close enough to distinguish words spoken in low tones, they heard a warning.

''Shoot!" he cried. ''There's a lot of bears under this tree!"

Although convulsed with laughter, the boys moved more cautiously after this. At last they came to the pine from which the voice proceeded. There was a rustle in the thicket as they advanced, and they saw a black object shambling away.

"There's Gilroy's flock of bears!" Jimmie shouted.

"And a little bit of a black bear at that," Ned laughed. "If Gilroy had made an ugly face at him, he'd have run away!"

The tree into which the fat confidential clerk had climbed was not a large one. In fact, it was swaying dangerously under his weight. As he moved his position at sight of the black back of the bear, the slender upshoot to which he clung gave way and he came clattering down through the few lower branches.

"Oh my! oh my! oh my!" he shouted. "I never should have come into this blasted country! I shall be eaten alive!"

Instead of rushing to Gilroy's assistance, his rescuers, boy-like, sat down on the mat of pine needles which strewed the ground and roared with laughter. Gilroy eyed them angrily without attempting to rise to his feet. His rage only made the scene more amusing.

"Why didn't you shoot him?" he demanded at length.

"Shoot him?" repeated Jimmie. "That bear is a great deal more freightened than you are.

At the rate of speed he's now going, he'll strike the arctic circle at exactly four-fifteen tomorrow morning!"

"He chased me up the tree," whined Gilroy. "He nipped at my heels as I left the ground, and I heard his teeth grinding together in the most frightful manner. I'll never get over this!"

"I guess he would have climbed the tree after you in about another minute," Jimmie declared, with a sly wink at Ned. "You see, it's just this way, Mr. Gilroy," he went on, "the bears out here are hungry for fat clerks from Wall street. I've heard they make stews of 'em," he concluded.

Gilroy now arose to his feet and stood gazing into the thicket in the direction of the bear's disappearance. Jimmie's assertion that bruin would hit the Arctic circle early the next morning seemed to give him great comfort. As the distance between the bear and himself increased, he grew braver and began throwing out his chest.

"What a chance that was for me to kill a bear!" he began, boastfully, "If I'd only had a gun with me, I might have had a fine rug made out of his hide! It would have been fine to show my friends."

"Sure it would!" declared Jimmie. "I'm

glad you didn't remember that you had a gun in your pocket. The bears out here are pretty sensitive about being shot at. If you'd blazed away at that cub, and hadn't shot him dead in his tracks the first time, he would have eaten you."

Gilroy put his hand to his pistol pocket and a look of pretended amazement came over his fat face.

"Upon my word!" he said, "I thought I left my gun in the bunk!"

"After this," Ned advised, "always keep your gun in sight when you go into the forest. Suppose there had been no tree to climb, what then?"

"I should have grappled with him, sir!" exclaimed Gilroy. "I certainly should have grappled with him."

"You would have had to catch him first," Jimmie grinned.

"How long since you left the camp?" Ned asked, after Jimmie had introduced the two.

"Perhaps half an hour ago," was the answer. "When I went to sleep, the boys were sitting by the fire, but when I woke there was no one in sight. I came out to look for them."

"I understand you came on a mission for Jack Bosworth's father?" asked Ned after a pause.

"Yes," was the reply, "at the request of my employer I came on this most dangerous mission. I shall be glad to see New York again."

Ned hesitated a moment and then asked:

"Did Mr. Bosworth ever say anything to you about a set of documents he wished us to bring to light?"

"He did not," was the answer.

"His purpose in sending you, then, was to secure, by means of our help, proof connecting a corporation he is fighting with unlawful acts which have been or may be committed in this section?"

"That is exactly the idea!" answered Gilroy.

"Come on," Jimmie shouted, "let's get back to camp. I begin to feel hungry already. Perhaps the boys have returned."

Before Gilroy would move out of the forest he insisted on pinning up certain rents in his clothing and combing out his mussed up hair with his fingers. There were also numerous scratches on his face, caused by contact with the rough branches of the tree, and these he thought necessary to nurse carefully with his handkerchief.

"Oh my!" laughed Jimmie, as the fat confidential clerk struggled under difficulties to make himself more presentable. "If you think you're in a muss, just look at this beautiful new khaki uniform I put on only a day or two ago! It's a peach, ain't it?''

''It certainly is in a mess,'' admitted Gilroy.

''Of course,'' grinned Jimmie. ''I fell down a chute, and rolled into the basement of a mountain, and climbed up a smutty chimney, and fell into a secret passage, and had all kinds of sport! Ned and I have had a glorious morning. You should have been with us.''

The confidential clerk frowned slightly, but made no reply.

When the boys reached the camp, after giving a great deal of mental and physical assistance to the clerk, they found it just as they had left it. The boys had not returned.

''Now, what kind of blockheads do you think they are to go away and leave the camp like this?'' Jimmie asked.

The boy did not know, of course, that his own signal, shown from the granite rock, had led to their departure, and also to their subsequent encounter with the half-breeds.

''We don't know why they left,'' Ned answered, ''but we must suppose that they had some good reason for doing so.''

''Do I understand,'' Gilroy asked, ''that something has happened to your companions?''

''All we know about it is that they're not here,'' replied Jimmie.

''There are altogether too many bears in this forest,'' suggested Gilroy. ''The lads may have encountered some of them.''

''That's a fact!'' laughed Jimmie. ''Perhaps we'd better go out and see if we can find a group of pine trees bearing a mess of Boy Scouts.''

''This is a serious matter,'' Ned interrupted. ''Judging from our own experiences, the boys may be having a bad time of it.''

''The outlaws are none too good to commit murder!'' Jimmie asserted.

## CHAPTER XI

### THE DEVIL'S PUNCH BOWL

"See here, boys," Frank Shaw suggested, as the three boys moved on through the forest, almost entirely surrounded by repulsive half-breeds, "this will be a fine story for Dad's newspaper. 'Captured by Bold, Bad Men; or, Why Little Frankie Didn't Get Home to His Beans'! That would be a fine title for the story, and I'll ask Dad to print a picture of three boys wandering through a jungle surrounded by a bunch of cheap skates that no decent dog would bark at."

"Keep still!" whispered Harry. "What's the use of stirring these people up? We're in no shape to scrap with them!"

"And then," Frank went on, "Dad might take a notion to send an expedition out here to round up these dirty greasers. If he does, I'm coming out just on purpose to see them hanged."

"Cut it out!" advised Jack.

"Of all the rotten, unwashed specimens of humanity I ever came across," Frank continued, speaking in a still louder tone, "this escort of ours takes the bun.    They're imitation bad-men all right.''

''A little of that goes a long way, young man,'' the leader of the party said.  ''It makes no difference to me what you say, but several of these men understand the English language and can speak it fluently.''

''I presume so,'' returned Frank.    ''I've seen just such a collection as that in jail in New York. Say, honest, Captain,'' he went on, ''if a bunch like this should run up against the strong-arm squad in New York, they'd get their heads beaten off just because of their ugly mugs.''

''Aw, what's the use!'' demanded Harry.

By this time several of the guards were casting ugly glances at Frank, who seemed to regard their disfavor with great joy.

''You'd better come on ahead and walk with me, young fellow,'' the leader said, taking Frank roughly by the arm and jerking him to a position in front.  ''If you get back there where those ugly ones are, they'll put a couple of bullets into your back and swear that you were trying to escape.''

On his way to the front of the party, Frank passed Jack and paused for a second only to whisper in his ear:

''Now, these ginks will be watching me every minute, waiting for a chance to shoot.   You may catch them off their guard directly and when you do, cut and run!''

''So that's what you did all the talking for?'' queried Jack.

''You bet!'' answered Frank. ''And while you're running, I'll do a little sprinting myself.''

''Here, you!'' shouted the leader, almost lifting Frank's feet from the ground as he dragged him away.

''What were you whispering to that boy?'' demanded one of the others.

''I was telling him,'' Frank answered, making an insulting face, ''that I used to have a dog that looked exactly like you.''

The fellow thus insulted sprang for the boy with upraised fist. The leader blocked his rush by imposing his own burly form, and the two went down together. The half-breeds sprang forward, too, the intention evidently being to assist their companion as against the leader.

Frank let out a yell which might have been heard half a mile away, and the three boys darted down the mountainside, followed by harmless shots from the guns of the half-breeds.

The incident had taken place on a rocky level flanked by steep slopes on each side. The place, in fact, was almost like a shelf of rock cut into a long fifty percent grade.

The ledge was narrow, and as the bunch clung

together where the leader and his opponent still struggled, one of them slipped over the edge of the declivity and started downward. Naturally he caught hold of the first object within his reach, and this happened to be the shoe of the outlaw nearest to him. This man, in turn, caught another, and two more tried to pull up the falling ones, with the result that in about half a minute five of the half-breeds were rolling and tumbling heels over head down the rocky slope.

The boys were not far out of their path, but they managed to elude the downrushing bodies as they swung by. Notwithstanding the gravity of the situation, the boys shrieked with laughter as the clumsy fellows went tumbling down, uttering vicious curses at the boys, at the mountain and at each other.

"I wish I had a gun now!" shouted Frank.

As he spoke a formidable weapon which seemed to be half revolver and half sawed-off shotgun, flew out of the hands of one of the involuntary acrobats and landed against Frank's side with a great thud.

Frank seized the weapon and backed away. By this time the leader was on his feet shouting wrathful commands for the boys to return.

"Easy, now," Frank shouted, moving away to the south. "If any of you ginks lift a finger until we get into the timber line, I'll empty this load of slugs into the thick of you."

The leader, more daring than the others, sprang down the slope, his great boots scattering fragments of rock and sending them hurtling down upon the heads of the half-breeds below. Frank was about to fire when the man lost his balance and joined the procession of those making for the bottom a la log.

"Here we go!" shouted Frank.

The boys raced along the slope until they came to a point of timber which, following a more fertile spot, thrust itself up the ascent. Here they disappeared, considering themselves reasonably safe in the seclusion of the forest. Frank examined his gun and found it empty.

"Good thing that dub didn't know it was empty!" he laughed.

"Don't stop now to throw bouquets at yourself!" grinned Harry.

"That's right!" Jack declared. "We want to be getting back to the camp. Gilroy 'll have a fit if he wakes up and finds us gone."

"Don't you ever think those half-breeds will give up the chase here," Frank suggested. "Do you know what they'll do?" he asked, "They'll circle around and get between us and the camp! That's what they'll do."

"I sometimes think," Harry snorted, turning

to Jack, "that Frank is getting so intelligent that he may have the gift of speech conferred upon him. He certainly has that proposition right."

"Well, if we can't go back to camp," Jack asked, "where can we go?"

"We'll have to glide into some gentle dell in the bosom of a friendly hill!" laughed Harry, "and send a scout out to watch those fellows spy upon the camp."

"If they've got a detachment of half-breeds guarding every squad of Boy Scouts that have strayed away from the camp today," Jack laughed, "they must have an army in here. Ned was coaxed away by a fake note; Jimmie went to find Ned and got lost himself, and we go out to answer a call for help and get mixed up with a lot of half-breeds. I guess we'll have to take a company of state troops with us next time we go camping."

"Well, let's be moving," urged Frank. "Those fellows' heads will be just sore enough when they quit rolling to shoot at anything in sight. They'd string us up if they caught us now."

In accordance with this reasoning, the boys turned south in the thicket then shifted to the east, then whirled back in a northerly direction. At one time they heard the shouts of the half-breeds on the slope far away to the south.

"They think we kept right on south," laughed Jack. "Now," he went on, "we'll walk north a long ways, climb the slope to the snow line, and come out on the camp from above. How's that strike you boys?"

"It listens good to me," Frank answered. "Do you suppose Ned is back there yet?" he continued.

"It struck me," Jack replied, "that the half-breeds we encountered were out looking for Ned or Jimmie."

"You'll have to guess again," Harry put in. "The ginks we encountered were stationed there to catch any Boy Scout who came in answer to that signal. That's some more of the work of that crooked messenger."

"Well, I hope the bears won't devour Gilroy while we're gone," Frank suggested. "It's likely to be night before we get back."

The boys walked for a long distance, and it was three o'clock by their watches when they turned up the slope. They would have felt less comfortable during the latter part of their journey if they had known that they were passing within a few hundred yards of the headquarters of the outlaws at the old mission.

After a time they came to what looked like a wrinkle in the face of the grand old mountain. They proceeded up this with no little caution, not knowing but enemies might be watching there. It was just such a place as outlaws lurking for prey or cowering from officers would be apt to seek. The wrinkle, or gully, led almost to the snow line and finally ended in a little dip which lay between two summits rising side by side, like jagged rows of teeth.

"I'm half starved and half frozen!" Harry declared, as he rested for a time in the depth of what had once been a mountain lake, but which had been drained by the gully. "If I ever get back in little old New York again, I'm going to get Dad to make me a gasoline buggy with a snout nine feet long, and I'm going to push traffic aside on Broadway for the next thousand years."

"How often have you said that?" laughed Jack.

"Let's see," Frank put in, "this is the twelfth trip we boys have taken, either in the interests of the Secret Service or on vacations, so this makes twelve times that Harry has promised never to leave New York again once he gets back there."

"That's all right!" Harry grinned. "You fellows ain't half so hungry as I am or you wouldn't feel so gay over it."

"Now, how far are we from camp?" asked Jack.

"About two miles on the level," Frank suggested, "and about four hundred miles the way the surface of the ground runs."

After a short rest the boys proceeded south, climbing over jutting spurs, dipping into depressions, and sliding over stony slopes until they were almost too tired to take another step.

"We'll get used to this in a month or two," Harry said, sitting plump down on a boulder.

Frank followed the boy's example, except that he stretched himself at full length, while Jack pushed on a few steps and stood peering over a rim of rock which lay directly in their way.

"Look here, boys!" Jack finally called. "You remember the place in Mexico called the Devil's Cauldron? Well, this is it!"

"What have you found now?" demanded Frank sleepily.

"Here's a round hole in the mountain," Jack answered back, "that you might hide a city block in. It's deep and the sides are almost smooth. Looks like the pit Kipling gets one of his characters in, only there's rock instead of sand."

The boys rose to their feet and looked over the ledge.

"And right there in the bottom," Harry exclaimed, "is a pool of water so clear that it looks like a diamond!"

"Running water, too," added Frank. "Now, where do you think that water comes from, and where does it go to?"

"Runs through a pass, foolish!" answered Jack.

"But there's no break in the formation," Frank insisted.

"Then it runs through a tunnel manufactured by itself!" Jack explained. "Anyway, it gets out somehow."

"What a dandy place to catch mountain trout!" shouted Harry.

"Yes, you get down there once and you'd think it was a dandy place!" laughed Frank. "You'd never get out in a hundred years."

"I'd like to see if there are fish there, anyway," suggested Harry. "I've heard so much about the firm flesh of fish caught in mountain streams that I'd like to investigate."

"Investigate nothing!" laughed Jack. "You'd starve to death there."

"Oh, that doesn't look so worse!" exclaimed Harry.

The boy leaned far over as he spoke. The stone upon which his breast pressed dropped away with a crash. The boy's heels flew into the air, and the next moment he was sliding down the awful declivity.

Jack and Frank heard the cry of terror as the boy disappeared and closed their eyes to shut out the horrible sight which they believed to be due the next instant.

## CHAPTER XII

### TREACHERY FEARED

"I would suggest," Gilroy remarked, as the boys stood in front of the barrier looking anxiously out in every direction, "that you prepare a bit of luncheon. I must confess that this mountain air gives me an appetite, and I had a light breakfast, you know."

"All right," Jimmie replied. "I'll build a fire, put on the big kettle and make a bear stew that will put an inch of fat on your ribs."

"A bear stew?" repeated Gilroy, holding up his white hands in horror.

"Sure, a bear stew."

"You don't mean to say that the ferocious creatures known as bears are served as food in this outrageous country, do you?"

"Certainly!" laughed Jimmie. "The bear is the noblest work of God when it comes to making a stew."

"I couldn't eat bear stew, indeed I couldn't," gasped Gilroy.

"All right," Jimmie said, "then we'll cook you some eggs."

The boy set to work preparing the stew. The

larder was well stocked with provisions, and he had plenty of vegetables and rice to use, so in a couple of hours he had a great kettle bubbling fragrantly over the fire. Gilroy was supplied with eggs and soda biscuit.

Leaving the confidential clerk munching his supper and looking about for bears, Ned and Jimmie walked around the corner of rock and stood looking over the fast-darkening landscape.

"I'll tell you what it is," Jimmie said, at length. "Those boys are in trouble somewhere. Its an even bet that they've been geezled by the ginks that grabbed us."

"I'm afraid you're right," Ned answered.

"Look here," Jimmie went on, in a moment. "I know the way to that old mission place. I could find my way there in the dark of the moon blindfolded. Now suppose I sneak over and see if there's any trace of the boys there or thereabouts?"

"We'd better wait a short time," Ned answered. "The outlaws in the subterranean rooms will naturally be doubly watchful after our sensational excape, and so we'd better wait until along in the night."

"They may not be there at all," Jimmie finally said. "They may be just lost in the mountains."

"I don't think they would really get lost," Ned decided.

While the boys talked around the angle of rock, a shrill cry followed by a pistol shot came from the camp.

In a moment Norman, the Boy Scout messenger boy, came dashing around the corner, white-faced and out of breath. He dropped down close to where the boys were standing and looked up at Ned with appealing eyes. He was evidently very much exhausted, for his breath came in short, hard gasps. There were spots of blood on his hands, as if they had been torn on rocky surfaces.

"Well?" asked Ned shortly. "What do you want here?"

Norman half arose and peered around the angle of rock.

"I came running up to the fire a minute ago," he said, still panting, "and some one in the cave shot at me as I passed."

"Don't you think you deserve shooting?" asked Ned.

"Shooting for what?" asked the other faintly.

"Because you have proven yourself a treacherous guide!" answered Ned.

"Aw, pitch him down the hill!" gritted Jimmie.

"Wait until I explain!" gasped Norman. "I have only a minute to spare."

"Well, what is it?" asked Ned.

"And get a new plot this time!" put in Jimmie. "Don't go to bringing out any old fake note!"

"You'll understand, some day," Norman said, lifting his eyes frankly to those of the boys. "You'll know all about it before long."

"Get down to business!" ordered Ned.

"Then listen," Norman went on. "Some of your friends are in trouble up near the summit."

"And you want us to follow you to the scene of activity!" laughed Jimmie. "That's almost as good as answering the note in person."

"Now listen to me," pleaded Norman.

"You worked that game once," roared Jimmie. "You got me geezled in the woods, and you got Ned lugged into the old mission."

"Let me tell you," Norman went on. "I was sent out into the mountains to look for you boys. I went off to the west because I didn't want to find you. I thought you wouldn't be in that direction."

"That's called 'bunk' in New York," Jimmie insisted.

"Let the boy have his say," Ned suggested.

"I went off to the west," continued Norman, "and walked a long way. I didn't want to go back to the mission at all, but I knew that if I didn't something serious would take place in New York."

"What do you mean by that?" asked Jimmie.

"I can't tell you," answered the boy. "I can only say that upon my keeping on good terms with Toombs and his gang depends the liberty and happiness of a person I am very fond of."

Jimmie snorted his disbelief, but Ned motioned for Norman to go on.

"When I got high up on the hill. I came to a depression known to the mountaineers as the Devil's Punch Bowl."

"Wasn't any punch in it, was there?" asked Jimmie, in derision.

"Just as I was about to turn away, I heard shouts from the bottom of the pit. I drew nearer to the edge and looked down. Two boys were beckoning and shouting to me to run for assistance."

"Two?" asked Ned anxiously.

"Only two," replied Norman. "There was another lying on the ground and he looked to me as if he might be dead."

"Why didn't you find out?" asked Ned.

"There is always quite a wind up on the mountains at this time of night," the boy answered, "and I couldn't understand all they said.  I understood, however, that they wanted me to come for you.''

''And you want us to go with you to this Devil's Punch Bowl, I presume,'' scoffed Jimmie.

''If you can find the place alone, I'll go back to the old mission,'' answered Norman.  ''It is not so very far away.''

''What sort of a place is this Devil's Punch Bowl?'' asked Ned, moving toward the cave and beckoning Norman to follow.

''It is just a deep pit between two ridges,'' was the answer.  ''It must be a hundred or more feet to the bottom.  The sides are so steep that escape from it is impossible.''

''It must be a dangerous place,'' Ned agreed.

''The mountaineers claim that no one ever left it alive,'' replied the boy with a very grave face.

''What ought we to take with us,'' asked Ned, ''in order to be of assistance to the boys? What do you suggest?''

''You must take plenty of ropes,'' was the answer.

Jimmie looked up into Ned's face appealingly.

''You're not going with this gink?'' he asked.

''I certainly am,'' replied Ned.  ''The boys may really be in trouble.''

''Then I'll go, too,'' Jimmie decided, ''but

I'll tell you right now that I don't believe a word of this story."

"Will you show the way?" asked Ned, bringing out a large coil of rope.

"Yes," was the reply, "if you'll treat me fairly while we're together. Some one shot at me from the cave as I came by."

Gilroy was now seen looking out of the cave. The firelight showed a set and frightened face.

"That's the boy!" he shouted, pointing a fat finger at Norman. "That's the boy that tried to sneak into the cave while you were away."

"That's the man that shot at me!" Norman said. "I guess he thought I was a burglar. I didn't try to get into the cave at all, but just looked over the barrier."

"I saw him trying to climb over!" shouted Gilroy.

"Never mind all that now," Ned advised. "If the boys really are in trouble we can't afford to lose any time getting to them."

"I'll give you another reason why you ought to hurry," Norman went on, "I've been gone from the camp quite a long time, and I don't know what's going on there, of course, but I can tell you right now that your camp will be watched tonight. There may be someone watching me now."

"What is the real object of all this?" asked

Ned. "We have nothing those fellows have use for, either information or documents of any kind."

"You probably couldn't make them believe that," suggested Norman. "At any rate," he went on, "if they believed what you say, they would still try to drive you out of the country."

"Had the outlaws anything to do with the plight in which you found the boys?" asked Jimmie.

"Certainly not!" was the reply. "When the boys escaped from the outlaws, they took the upper route back to your cave and came upon the Devil's Punch Bowl. My idea is that one fell in and that the others, in some manner, worked their way down to the bottom and attempted to get him out. They didn't say so, but that's the way it looked to me."

"So the half-breeds captured the boys, did they?" Jimmie asked.

"Yes," was the reply. "Some one sent up a Boy Scout help signal in the forest below here, and the boys must have gone to see what it meant. The half-breeds were wandering around there and captured them, but the boys got away by some trick or other and took to the mountain."

Jimmie stood looking at Ned with a shamed face.

"Say!" he said, "I made that Boy Scout signal, just before those ginks started to march me off to the old mission. I never thought our boys would take any notice of it. I guess I'm to blame for all this trouble, Ned. I must be getting awful dense, never to remember that our boys were looking for just such signs at the time I left the camp."

"I saw the signal," Norman said, "and answered it. I was cooking in front of Toombs' tent when the two columns of smoke showed and I built another fire on the plea that I needed two to cook the dinner. The fires didn't make much smoke, so I soaked some of the wood I put on."

"And I saw your signal, too," Jimmie explained, "and started toward it. That's the time the half-breeds gave me the pinch."

"Now," said Ned, turning to Norman, "we're going to leave Gilroy, the man who mistook you for a burglar, here to watch the camp while we go to the assistance of the boys. I don't think you'd better go with us. We may come upon a bunch of the outlaws and have to fight. If with us, you would be recognized and that would end your usefulness so far as we are concerned.

"I'm afraid I can't help you any more," Norman said hesitatingly. "It would be terrible if the news got back to New York that

I had turned traitor to Toombs. I can't endure the thought!"

"What would happen?" asked Jimmie. "Why don't you speak plainly?"

"I can't tell you what would happen," the boy answered. "It is something I don't even dare think about."

"Then of course you can't afford to accompany us to the Devil's Punch Bowl," Ned said, "and I was about to suggest that you remain here with Gilroy for a short time after our departure."

"Aw, let Gilroy take care of himself!" Jimmie said.

Ned laughed as he threw a long coil of rope over his shoulder and provided himself with a couple of electric flashlights.

"Gilroy," he said, "would be having three fits at a time if he knew that we are leaving him here alone in the night. If the boy will remain a short time until we get out of sight and hearing, that will help matters materially. You'll stay will you?" he added.

"Only a few minutes," answered Norman.

"And if there is to be a raid on the camp to-night," Ned went on, "perhaps you may be able to warn us in time."

"I can't promise that," the boy said. "I can't take any chance on offending Mr. Toombs.

I know that he's a dirty trickster, and that he means mischief to you boys, but I've said all I dare say."

The boy entered the cave and engaged in converstion with Gilroy, in accordance with Ned's instructions, and Ned and Jimmie, who had in the meantime received definite instructions as to the location of the Devil's Punch Bowl, started up the steep slope of the mountain.

"Suppose the boy is lying?" asked Jimmie anxiously.

## CHAPTER XIII

### AT THE BOTTOM OF THE BOWL

Jack and Frank stood at the edge of the Devil's Punch Bowl with their hearts beating wildly, listening for the dreaded sound which they knew must come from below. However, no such sound came, and presently they found the courage to cast their eyes down the steep incline.

Far down, at the very bottom of the pit, lying close to the edge of the pool of water which had been observed before, they saw Harry, lying perfectly motionless. He had fallen at least a hundred feet.

"It's terrible!" Frank faltered. "I wish we had never come into the mountains! I wish we had never seen California."

"He may not be dead," suggested Jack.

"Not dead!" repeated Frank. "Not dead after a fall like that?"

"I'm not going to give up hope until I'm sure!" Jack answered stoutly.

The two boys stood for a moment gazing down the tremendous fall, and then cast their eyes over the landscape in every direction.

''What are you looking for?'' asked Jack.

''Something that will help us lower into the pit.''

''If we only had a long rope,'' Jack wailed.

''Well, we haven't got any long rope,'' Frank replied, ''and we've just got to get down there. We've got to find a way.''

''I have been thinking,'' Jack stated after a moment's thought, ''that we might possibly work our way downward by circling about the pit.''

''You mean wind ourselves down like a corkscrew?'' asked Frank.

''That's it exactly!''

''Why, the walls are almost perpendicular!'' Frank asserted. ''We never can get down there in the world!''

''Then we'll have to hasten back to camp and get a rope,'' said Jack.

''I just can't go away and leave Harry lying there like that!'' exclaimed Frank. ''I just can't do it. We've got to get down into that devil's hole in some way. It may be difficult but we've got to do it.''

''If we could only get over to the other side,'' Jack said, ''we might be able to work our way down a part of the distance. It seems to me that the rock is rougher there, and the side not quite so steep.''

"It does look that way," Frank answered, "and I think we'd better try to get over there. It will help some, even if we can't get clear to the bottom. We can at least find out whether Harry is alive."

"I'll never leave him lying there, alive or dead!" exclaimed Jack.

The boys at once set out on a difficult journey toward the far side of the Devil's Punch Bowl. In many places they had only a rim of rock less than six inches in diameter for a foot-hold. On one side, hundreds of feet above them stretched the snow-covered summit, while on the other side lay the precipice dipping into the Devil's Punch Bowl. At last, after great exertion and very many narrow escapes, the boys reached the desired location and looked about.

"We ought to be able to get down from this side," Frank said. "You stand here at the top of the rim and let me down arm's length. You see that shelf there? Oh, it's not more than two inches wide," the boy went on, as Jack looked his astonishment, "but I can stand on it all right by leaning against the face of the wall.

"Well, I can reach that with my toes if you'll let me down steadily. Then you drop down the full length of your arms and I'll keep you from falling when you strike the ledge. There are other ledges below and so we may be able to get clear to the bottom.''

''I'm afraid!'' Jack said. ''I'm afraid I'll push you off the ledge when I drop down.''

''We've got to take the chance!'' Frank returned. ''We've just got to take the chance, and that's all there is to it. We can't let Harry lie there. We're going to get him out, alive or dead.''

''All right!'' Jack said. ''Drop your legs inside the pit and catch hold of my hands and I'll let you down. We can only try!''

It was indeed a desperate undertaking. The walls of the Devil's Punch Bowl, as all who have ever visited that section understand, are almost perpendicular three-fourths of the way down. Then they form almost a perfect bowl—at least, the bottom of a perfect bowl. In the center of this bowl lies, or did lie at that time, a pool of clear, pure water.

For an instant Frank groped blindly, his feet swinging out into the awful chasm, and then he found the ledge which he had mentioned. He looked up to see Jack looking with face red from exertion over the rim.

''Now, chum,'' he said, ''swing yourself in and slide down. The eighty per cent slope will throw your weight away from the pit and I'll keep you from tumbling backwards when you strike the ledge.''

"That ledge doesn't look very solid to me," Jack suggested.

''You couldn't break it with an axe!'' replied Frank. ''It is safe enough, and the slope will keep your body on the ledge if you don't get scared. Now go to it, old boy!''

Frank talked bravely enough, but he held his breath as Jack came sliding down. When the boy's feet struck the ledge, he certainly would have tumbled backward into the pit if Frank had not thrown one arm against him. The boys looked at each other for a moment without speaking. They fully understood the peril they were in, yet they tried to be cheerful, each seeking to belittle the danger to the other.

''There,'' Frank said lightly, ''that was easy enough. We'll never get any medals for doing an easy stunt like that.''

''Of course, it was easy,'' Jack answered, ''and the next ledge is not so far away and is broader. We'll have to slide down there together side by side and then if you fall, I can give you a lift, and you can do the same for me. I don't think we're going to have so much trouble with this old hole after all. Lots of things look easy after the start.''

''That's always the way in this gay old world

of ours," Frank answered, "all you got to do is to face a dreaded thing and half its terror is lost."

The next ledge was easily reached, but was not so safe as the other, the edge having crumbled away to some extent. In fact, the boys slid off a great deal quicker than they would otherwise have done, as the rock under their feet gave indications of dropping.

And so, working their way from ledge to ledge, sometimes at the peril of their lives, sometimes finding the way fairly safe and easy, the boys reached a point not more than twenty feet from the spot where their unconscious chum was lying.

"Now," Jack said as they stood on the last ledge and looked into the clear pool below, "we've got to slide down here like we were going down a chute. The chances are that we won't have any neat uniforms when we get to the bottom, and the possibility is that we'll be good and wet by the time we make our way out of that pool."

"I'm not going into that pool!" Frank declared. "It's colder than Greenland up here now, and if we get wet we'll be frozen stiff in half an hour. We can't do Harry any good by going to him in a condition calling for nurses and hot drinks."

"I don't know how you're going to help tumbling into the pool!" Jack answered. "It lies not more than twenty feet from the bottom of the incline."

"I'll show you how!" Frank declared. "All you've got to do is to slide down on your little empty tummy and wear your fingers up to the second or third joint digging into the rocks."

"I ain't going to wear out any fingers!" Jack insisted. "You remember that great big jack-knife? The one you said ought to cause my arrest for carrying concealed weapons? Well, I've got that jack-knife with me right now. I'm going to break the big blade off short and dig into the rock with that all the way down!"

"What do you want to break the blade off for?" asked Frank.

"So I can get my hand close to the point of contact without cutting my fingers off," replied Jack.

"I wish I had a knife like that," Frank said, regretfully.

"Well," Jack proposed in a moment, "we can bunch in together and each one can have a hand on the knife. Say, but won't that be a jolly proposition? Wearing out a perfectly good Boy Scout uniform on the dirty old rocks of the Devil's Punch Bowl?"

"Any way to get down to the bottom!" Frank declared.

The plan figured out by Jack worked to perfection, and the boys reached the edge of the pool without tumbling in. Still, however, they were not within reach of the spot where their chum was lying.

During all this time, Harry had shown not the slightest evidence of life. Crumpled up as from a fatal blow, the boy lay exactly in the position into which he had fallen.

"We made the slide on the down-grade, all right. Now I wish we could slide up over the spur that separates us from the side of the pool where Harry is." Jack said.

"All we've got to do is to climb," Frank answered. "I never saw any ledge of rock, or any body of water, or any trouble of any kind, that you could wish yourself over."

"And the sooner we get there, the better!" Jack declared.

The boys were very pale now, for the time was near at hand when they were to know the truth concerning the condition of their chum.

They made their way over the spur which shot out of the lower wall and down to the pool with no little difficulty, and at last stood at the edge of the water where Harry lay, his face turned upward to the sky, his arms lying limply at his sides.

The boys hesitated an instant before bending over him.

"I'm afraid!" Jack whispered.

"I'm afraid, too!" Frank replied, covering for an instant his face with his hands. "I'm afraid he's dead!"

Then Jack bent closer and fixed his eyes keenly on the boy's face.

"Say!" he said excitedly. "Look here, Frank, Harry is actually breathing! He may not be fatally wounded after all!"

Frank shook his head but hastened to the pool of water and brought back as much as his hat would hold. This he threw into the face of the prostrate boy and then both stood waiting and watching with their hearts beating wildly.

"He's coming to!" shouted Frank in a moment. "He certainly is coming to! Now what do you think of that after a tumble of a hundred feet!"

"It couldn't have been a straight drop!" Jack declared. "He would have been smashed all to flinders!"

"Don't mention it," Frank cried, "you give me the shivers!"

Directly Harry's eyes opened and he looked painfully about.

"Hello, old Scout!" shouted Frank.

"Are you getting hungry?" demanded Jack.

A faint smile flickered over the face of the injured lad, and he closed his eyes again.

"I'm going to know something more about this!" Jack insisted. "Can you hear, Harry?" he asked after a short pause.

Harry nodded and Jack took him tenderly by one leg.

"Yell, when I hurt," he said.

He moved the limb up and down, sideways, too, but only a smile came to the boy's lips. That leg was evidently all right.

"Now for the other one!" Jack declared hopefully. "If I hurt you just give me a kick with your well hoof!"

That leg was all right, too. In a moment, Harry stirred one arm faintly and then lifted it to his face.

"And one arm's all right, too!" almost shouted Frank. "Say, kid," he continued, "how did you ever negotiate that tumble and not get broken into little pieces?"

Harry opened his eyes again and smiled faintly.

"I slid down most of the way," he said. "My left arm is broken, and I've got a bump on my dome big enough to hide a cow in, but I guess that's about all. How's that for luck?"

"Luck?" repeated Jack. "If you'd fall into the Polar sea, you'd find a pot of boiling water!'

"I won't believe you're all right except one broken arm," Frank insisted, "until I see you sitting up and taking notice."

Harry sat up weakly and looked around.

"Well," he said in a feeble voice, "you boys got down here all right. Now, how are you ever going to get out?"

## CHAPTER XIV

### A BIT OF ENGINEERING

"You're right, there, Harry!" Frank answered. "You stated the question before the house correctly!"

"Oh, we'll get out some way," Jack insisted. "We're not going to stay in this little old hole forever. It's too cold here."

"Can you walk, Harry?" asked Frank.

"In a short time, probably," was the reply. "While I'm resting, you boys chase around and see if there's any chance of getting back to the surface of the earth again."

Frank and Jack spent some time walking about the edge of the pool but could find nothing that looked like an exit.

"If I could turn myself into a barrel of water," Jack stated with a whimsical smile, "I could run out!"

"Yes, and if you could change yourself into a bird," Frank laughed, "you could fly out. But you're not fluid, and you haven't got wings, so I guess we've got to find some other way."

"Speaking about water," Jack mused, "how

does the water get out of here? It seems to come from springs in the sides of the pool as well as from rills down the mountainside when the snow melts. If it didn't get out in some way, the Devil's Punch Bowl would simply be a mountain lake. Perhaps we can get through the passage made by the water."

Following this suggestion, the boys passed around the pool a number of times always dodging the handle-like spur which shot into the basin by turning back, and finally came to a whirlpool on the east side which showed the drop in the water. The boys examined the whirl of water earnestly.

"Is the hole which makes this whirlpool clear down to the bottom?" asked Jack.

"It isn't more than four feet from the surface," answered Frank. "It runs in the wall."

You can see it, can you?" asked Jack.

"Plainly," was the reply. "It's as large as a church door."

"It wouldn't be safe to dive in there and swim through, would it?"

"I should say not!" replied Frank. "The passage is entirely filled by the current and you couldn't breathe in there more than half a minute. Besides all that, the swiftness of the current shows a steep fall and you'd probably bump your head against a rock before you went a hundred feet. Nothing doing in that line, kid!''

Again and again the boys tramped around the edge of the pool, stopping whenever they came to Harry's side to speak words of encouragement, but all they discovered in the way of an exit was a crevice which might at one time have furnished an exit for the waters.

The wash from the rocks, brought down, undoubtedly, by water from the melting snows, had apparently lifted the margin of the pool at least a yard above the mouth of the old crevice, which was something like a foot in width. This accumulation of pulverized rock formed a perfect and complete dam across the mouth of the opening.

''Here's a dry exit,'' Frank exclaimed with a grim smile. ''If we could just whittle off a few pounds of fat, we might be able to get through there!''

''It dips down pretty fast,'' Jack answered. ''The chances are that we'd get about such a bump as Harry received before we found the sunshine again. Well, it's not large enough anyway,'' he added, ''so we may as well look for some other means of egress.''

While the boy was still standing by the crevice looking about with hopeful eyes, Frank caught sight of a moving object on the rim above.

"Now, what do you suppose that is?" he asked.

In a moment, Jack's eyes rested on the object, too.

"It's a boy!" he said. "A boy all right enough, and it's peaches to prunes that he's the chap who's been playing villian ever since we came into the mountains. I wish he had with him the rope that he will eventually be hanged with."

"Hush!" replied Frank with a grimace. "Keep it dark! Don't you ever tell him that he's going to be hanged. If you do, he won't ever help us out of this blooming old punch bowl."

The boy stood looking down into the bowl for a moment, listening to the shouts for assistance which the boys now sent up, made a few quick signals, and turned away.

As the reader understands, the assistance Norman sought to give the boys could best be rendered by seeking their friends and informing them of the situation. Jack and Frank were, of course, greatly enraged at the boy's seemingly heartless desertion of them.

"Now what do you think of that for a cold-blooded reptile?" demanded Jack. "That fellow certainly is the limit!"

"You just wait," Frank shouted, almost dancing about in his anger, "you just wait till I get my hands on that gink. I'll change his face so his friends won't know him. The idea of his going off and leaving us in such a fix as this!"

"It's rotten!" Jack agreed.

"Rotten?" echoed Frank, "it's worse than rotten! It's stinking mean!"

"Which reminds me," Jack went on, "that if we ever get out of here we've got to accomplish the exit by our own exertions."

"You talk like you had a suggestion to make," Frank declared.

"I have!" answered Jack. "You see that crevice in the edge of the Punch Bowl, don't you? Well, that used to carry away the waters of the pool. Some day the water became stuffed with sand and the pool found another way out."

"I begin to understand!" Frank exclaimed. "I think I know what you mean. You have an idea that we can restore the water to its old channel and creep out through the larger passage, like the Egyptians crossing the Red Sea without getting their feet wet?"

"That's the idea," Jack exclaimed, "that's just the idea! Only the Egyptians didn't cross the Red Sea without getting their feet wet. It was the Hebrew children who crossed between two vertical walls of water.   The Egyptians got their's right there in the mud!''

''Have it your own way,'' Frank laughed. ''I'm afraid I don't remember my Sunday School lessons very well.   Have it your own way, only plan some escape from this everlasting pit.''

''Just as I was about to say when you interrupted with your fake story about the Egyptian army,'' Jack went on, ''we may be able in time to cut through the natural levee that separates the waters of the pool from the old channel.   If we can, we can draw the water out of the present exit and use it for our own escape.''

''That's the idea!'' Frank declared.

The two boys now made a closer inspection of the natural levee and the mouth of the crevice. They discovered that by cutting through a couple of feet of sand, the distance being about ten feet, they could, indeed, turn the waters of the pool into its old channel.

Of course this would not provide a depth of channel sufficient to empty the pool, but they believed that, with the natural wash of the current, the surface might be lowered so that water would no longer find its way into the large opening.

Working with such bits of sharp-edged shale as they could find, the boys fell to their task without delay.   Harry, observing their industry from a distance, smiled happily at the thought that the boys had at least found a way out which was worth considering.

"If we just had a couple of shovels like those muckers use over on the East river," Jack said, wiping the sweat from his forehead with the sleeve of his jacket, "we could cut through this obstruction in about five minutes. This is a fierce game!"

"I'm getting so I like these strenuous moments," Frank declared, putting both hands to his aching back. "The fact of the matter is," he went on, "that I'd rather be at work draining the Devil's Punch Bowl than playing the part of a little sissy cigar-store boy in New York."

"I'm glad you like it!" Jack replied, sourly.

It was almost dark when at last the trench was completed. It was with great satisfaction that the boys saw the water trickle into the new channel and find its way to the crevice. As the current grew stronger, it washed the banks away, and in a very short time a roaring torrent was rushing into the old outlet.

"That's the idea!" Frank exclaimed. "There's a head of water here that ought to cut that channel six feet deep," he went on. "And that will give us a dry tunnel to walk out of."

"To walk into," corrected Jack. "We don't know whether we'll ever walk out of it or not."

"Well, you needn't tell that to Harry!" exclaimed Frank reproachfully. "We've got to make him believe that it's a sure thing we can get him out of this rotten old excavation in the hills."

"And we're going to do it, too!" declared Jack. "I don't know just how we're going to do it, but we're going to do it! The channel will soon be dry enough for us to investigate, and somewhere is better than nowhere—by which I mean this hole in the rocks."

Hearing the rushing water, Harry arose to a sitting position and looked over toward his chums with a smile on his pale face.

"I knew you could do it!" he shouted, still in a faint voice. "I knew you would find a way."

"You bet we'll find a way!" Jack answered. "We've been in worse holes than this and always got out!"

"Now you've said something!" Frank declared.

The boys watched the running water, every moment gaining in force, for a long time, and then, just as the last rays of the sun touched the snowy mantle of the mountain, the water passed below the level of a large opening and they saw it drying out.

"That's what Grant did at Vicksburg," Frank laughed. "When he found the water occupying the channel he wanted to use himself, he just turned it to one side."

"That's exactly what we've done here," Jack agreed, "but now that we have turned it aside, there's a question as to whether we can make the same use of the channel.

"The only way to find out is to go to it," Frank advised. "Did those ginks take away your searchlight?"

"They did not," was the reply. "They took away my revolver and looked at the searchlight, but the latter they passed back to me because it seemed to be worthless as a weapon and bulky to carry."

"I've got mine, too," Frank said, "if it isn't smashed."

The boys examined their electrics with great care, and, to their great satisfaction, found that they were still fit for use.

It was now so dark that the lights were actually needed in the pit, still they did not turn them on, fearful that the boy who had shown himself for an instant and then disappeared might return with the half-breeds.

"The first thing to do," Jack suggested, "is to bring Harry over to the mouth of this dry channel. You see," he went on, "we've got to investigate the place before we attempt to carry him in, and he'll feel better if we place him where he can hear our voices and see our lights. I guess we can carry him so as not to cause him suffering or injure his bruises."

"I'll just bet he can walk over," Frank declared. "Anyway, I know he won't like the idea of being carried around like a baby."

On being consulted upon the point, Harry declared that he could walk just as well as not, and walk he did, although his steps were rather shaky at first. The entrance to the tunnel was quite large, tapering away as it mined the hill. Into this large outer chamber, for such it virtually was, Harry was seated with one of the searchlights for company, and Frank and Jack proceeded on their tour of investigation.

For the first few feet they were able to walk with their backs only slightly bent but then they advanced slowly on their hands and knees. When at last they reached a steep declivity extending, apparently, far into the heart of the mountain, they turned back and brought the wounded boy up to that place.

"Now keep your light covered," Jack advised, "and if anyone comes down to the pit led by that thief of a boy messenger, they will naturally think we had made a get-away."

"We're going down this long incline," Frank went on, "and when we get to the bottom, if everything is clear, we're coming back after you."

For a time the voices and lights of the boys supplied companionship for the wounded lad, then they were heard and seen no more.

Harry waited for a long time for some sign of the return of his friends, but they did not come and he feared the worst.

## CHAPTER XV

### THE TROUBLES OF GILROY

Following carefully the directions given them by Norman, Ned and Jimmie toiled up the slope until they came to the summit of the ridge which lay along the side of the Sierra Nevadas and then turned to the north. The way was steep and rocky, but in their anxiety and excitement they made good progress.

''The boy may be lying,'' Ned replied in answer to Jimmie's question, ''but we can't take that for granted. We've just got to go and see if the boys are in such a predicament as he described.''

''At first,'' Jimmie announced, ''I had rather a good opinion of Norman. But lately I've been thinking over all the tricks he has played on us, and I'm becoming convinced that he is a bad egg.''

''The record does look rather black,'' Ned answered. ''Every time we have listened to advice or suggestions from him, we have gotten into trouble. He has always told a good story, and we have always had the worst of it. If this proves true in the present case, we will settle with him the next time he comes across our path.''

''You don't suppose they'll go to the camp and stir up Gilroy, do you?'' asked Jimmie after a long time.

''If they do, he'll be scared out of his skin!'' Ned laughed.

''What made me ask,'' Jimmie went on, ''is that I saw lights flashing back there, and I thought I heard some one calling.''

''You must be mistaken!'' Ned insisted.

''Now just come over here and look for yourself,'' Jimmie answered. ''Here's an elevation, something like the one I stood on when I saw the commotion and heard the voice at the camp. Come on over and see what you can make of it.''

Ned stepped to the elevation occupied by his chum and looked out over the slope of the mountain. From where he stood the entrance to the cave was not in sight, it being concealed by the dip of the rock in which the cavern lay. However, a short distance up the slope, he saw a light moving and heard the call of a frightened voice.

''There!'' Jimmie exclaimed triumphantly. ''What do you make of that?''

''Perhaps the boys have returned,'' suggested Ned. ''Perhaps they are calling to us now not to wander off in search of them.  Suppose we wait here a minute and see?''

''That ain't any of our boys putting up a roar like that!'' Jimmie insisted.  ''I'll bet a dollar its that fat old confidential clerk.  Say, Ned!'' he went on, ''that fellow has got more screech in him than any full-grown man I ever saw.  Do you mind how he cut the air with his agony when the bear had him up the tree?''

''It certainly is Gilroy!'' Ned exclaimed impatiently.  ''Now, what do you suppose sent him up here after us?''

''He probably found himself alone,'' suggested Jimmie, ''and wandering out, saw our light.  I remember of flashing one when we passed around that big boulder.''

''He's coming on like an insane man!'' said Ned angrily.  ''If there's an enemy within ten miles of us, he will have no difficulty in locating us after this.  I wish I could stop him.''

Ned did not in the least overstate the case when he said that Gilroy was coming on like an insane person.  After finding himself alone in the cave, the fat clerk had seized a searchlight and dashed out in quest of the boys.  As Jimmie had suggested, he had seen a flash of light up the slope and followed on.

As he advanced now, puffing so that his approach might be heard many rods away, he swung the light frantically in the air and called out at the top of his voice. With an exclamation of impatience, Ned turned on his own light and ran toward him.

''Keep still!'' he shouted as soon as the voice of the clerk gave him an opportunity to cut in. ''Keep still, I tell you! You'll have every robber and murderer in the mountain down on us!''

"And now its robbers and murderers, is it?" shrieked the clerk. ''It was bears and panthers down in the cave. 1 saw a bear sneaking up to the provision box just as I left. He seemed to want to eat me!''

By this time Jimmie had joined the two, and now stood with a grin on his freckled face, rather enjoying the situation.

''And you chased off and left him chewing up our grub, did you?'' he demanded. ''What are we going to eat tomorrow?''

''Oh my! oh my!'' wailed Gilroy. ''I don't believe there will ever be any tomorrow. Once I get out of this brutal country, I'll never leave New York again!''

"What are we going to do with him, Ned?" asked Jimmie.

"He's simply got to go back to the cave," Ned answered. ''We can't have him with us at a time like this.''

"I can't go back to the cave!" shouted Gilroy, again brandishing his searchlight in the air. "I won't go back to the cave alone!" he continued. "If you insist on my leaving you, I'll start afoot over the mountains for San Francisco."

"If you should do a fool thing like that," Jimmie declared, "the bears would have a beautiful feast of fat clerk before morning!"

"I won't go back to the cave, I just won't!" insisted Gilroy.

"Well," Ned said hesitatingly, "if you'll keep your eyes open and your mouth closed, and hand me that light so you won't be showing it every second, you may come along with us."

Gilroy meekly handed over the electric, and the three proceeded on their way, Ned walking close to the fat clerk in order to ensure his silence. Jimmie trailed along with a grin on his face.

Finally Ned paused and pointed to two parallel ridges to the north.

"There," he said, "unless I am very much mistaken, are the ridges which stand on either side of the Devil's Punch Bowl."

"Then we'll soon know whether that messenger is a liar or not," Jimmie stated. "He may be all right, but, just the same, I'm looking for some one to butt in on us every minute now!"

They were not molested, however, as they

walked along, winding into gulches, climbing to the top of crags, and occasionally making their way over narrow ledges. Gilroy actually shivered as the boys forced him along, sometimes leading him by the arm, at other times pushing him along with many sly winks and chuckles.

There was only the light of the stars, but the ridges were clearly outlined because of the stretches of snow which cloaked them.

At last they came to the verge of the pit and looked down.

"This is the place, sure enough!" Ned decided. "Unless the boy who gave the information is an accomplished liar, we ought to find our chums at the bottom of this wicked old precipice."

Gilroy stood for a moment trembling on the edge of the cavern and then almost dropped back into Ned's arms.

"We'll never get down there, never!" he wailed. "We'll drop off into space and never see the Great White Way again."

"Go to it, partner!" grinned Jimmie, not a little disgusted at the lack of physical courage exhibited by the fat clerk. "Get your troubles all off your chest and then cheer up. The worst is yet to come!"

Gilroy sat flat down at the lip of the Devil's

Punch Bowl and almost sobbed out his grief and fright.

"If I ever get out of this rotten old country," he declared, "I'll lock myself up in a steam-heated flat, and remain there as long as I live!"

Leaving the fat clerk bewailing his fate, Jimmie made his way to where Ned was standing, looking anxiously down into the depression.

"Do you see anything of the boys?" he asked.

"Not a thing," Ned replied. "The fact of the matter is," he went on, "that we couldn't distinguish a flock of white elephants down there. It's darker than a pocket!"

"Then what are we going to do?" demanded Jimmie. "The boy didn't lie about the locality, but it may be that he lied about the lads being here. Anyway," he went on, "we've got to make our way down this wicked old drop and find out whether they're here or not."

The narrow ledges down which Jack and Frank had made their way were now out of sight because of the darkness. In fact, to the boys looking into the black hole from above, there seemed no possible way of entering the place where they believed their chums to be.

While they stood there, wondering how the downward journey was to be made in safety even with the rope, the round eye of an electric searchlight became visible at the mouth of the channel from which the water had been led away. Jimmie pointed to it eagerly.

"They are there!" he cried excitedly. "There they are, sure enough!"

"It must be the boys," Ned replied, "because that finger of light comes from an electric torch-light, and, so far as I know, we are the only ones having them here."

"Then this Norman kid told the truth for once in his life!" Jimmie admitted. "If he really has directed us to the assistance of our friends I'll forgive him all the mean things he ever did to us."

"Well," Ned said in a moment, "we can now try the rope. We don't know whether it is long enough to reach the bottom or not, but it will at least bring us nearer to our chums. I don't half like the idea of going down in the darkness, because there's no knowing what we may run into, but it's got to be done all the same."

"Let me go!" exclaimed Jimmie excitedly. "You and Gilroy can stay here and handle the rope."

"But you always get lost, little boy!" Ned said with a chuckle.

"I don't know how I'm ever going to get lost in the bottom of a dip like that," Jimmie answered. "From what I can see of it, it looks about like the bottom of an old brass kettle."

After listening to the conversation of the boys for a moment, and reaching the conclusion that he would be required to drop into the dark pit with the others, Gilroy now sprang to his feet and approached Ned with trembling footsteps.

"I can't get down there!" he almost shouted. "My arms are weak, and my shoulders are lame, and I never could hang onto the rope. I should fall and be crushed to a pulp on the rocks below!"

"Look here, Gilroy!" Ned said angrily. "You must remember that we have troubles of our own. If you don't want to go with us, perhaps you may be able to find your way back to camp."

"Never, never, never!" cried the fat confidential clerk. "Didn't I tell you that I left a bear at the camp?"

"Well," Ned argued with the fellow, "you and I will lower Jimmie into the hole. Then you can lower me and wait until we get ready to come back. I'll leave a revolver and searchlight with you, only you mustn't do any shooting, and you mustn't show the light under any circumstances. It would be dangerous to do so."

"You'll be sure to come back?" pleaded Gilroy. "It would be a wicked thing to do to leave me here in the darkness!"

"Aw, of course we'll come back!" interrupted Jimmie. "We've got to come back, for there's no other way to get out of the gloomy old den."

Gilroy seemed to be more cheerful over this arrangement, and assisted quite capably in lowering Jimmie over the lip of the precipice. The two passed out the rope to the boy dangling at the lower end until the cord was almost entirely unwound. Then a call from below announced to them that the lad had found footing.

"Now then," Ned explained to the confidential clerk, "when the rope is drawn up, you lie down on your stomach on the other side of the ledge so that you may by no possibility be drawn down. Pay out the rope slowly till I tell you that I have reached bottom and then leave it dangling over the edge. We may have to make a quick jump for it, you know," he added. "In that case, we want it handy."

Gilroy's teeth fairly chattered at the thought of being left alone with such a responsibility, but he said nothing, and Ned soon stood by Jimmie's side at the bottom of the precipice.

"Have you seen any more lights?" the boy asked.

"Nary a light," was the reply, "but I thought once that I heard voices coming from the spot in which the illumination was seen."

"Then we may as well be moving in that direction," Ned observed, and directly the two boys found themselves gazing at the opening from which the water had been recently drained.

## CHAPTER XVI

### A FALL IN THE NIGHT

Becoming too anxious for the safety of his friends to remain seated in the position in which he had been left, Harry at last arose to his feet and advanced down the passage toward the incline where they had disappeared.  He could see nothing, and presently turned back.

Instead of sitting down again, he moved back, always painfully because of his broken arm, toward the entrance to the old tunnel. He remembered faintly that Jack and Frank had called out to some one at the top of the pit during the afternoon, and his hope was now that whoever had visited the place and witnessed their plight would return.

He reached the entrance and flashed his light about eagerly.  No one was in sight and he turned back disheartened.  Had he known that the finger of light from the electric had been seen by Ned and Jimmie, he would have returned to his old position with a much lighter heart.

The discouraged boy sat down at the head of the incline to once more watch and listen for the return of his chums.   His broken arm was now becoming very painful, and at last he turned on the electric with a view of rearranging the rough sling in which Frank and Jack had placed it.

The boys had been too anxious at the moment of reaching the bottom of the pit to attempt the setting of the limb at that time.   They might have done so had they realized that an hour or two must elapse before they could reach a place more suitable for the undertaking.

The instant the boy turned on the light, he heard a shout from the rear, and turning, he saw two flashlights moving toward him.   At first the figures behind the lights were not discernible, but as they came nearer he recognized the forms of Ned and Jimmie.   The boys approached him almost gaily.   Norman had reported Harry lying inertly at the bottom of the Devil's Punch Bowl, and they had in a measure prepared their minds to find the boy dead or fatally injured.

So, when they saw him leaning against the wall of the old channel, arranging the handkerchief sling which sustained his broken arm, they almost shouted with joy.   In a moment they were at his side.

"Hiding, eh?" exclaimed Jimmie, his voice almost choking with emotion.   "You thought we couldn't find you, did you?"

"Are you badly hurt?" was Ned's first question.

"Just a broken arm," Harry answered trying to speak very calmly, although the pain was now excruciating.

"Where are Frank and Jack?" was the next question.

Harry pointed toward the sloping passage.

"Trying to find a way out," he answered.

"Were they here when you fell?" asked Jimmie. "If they were, why didn't they set your broken arm? They understand first aid to the injured just as well as we do. Now, you drop right back on this nice, soft bed of granite and I'll see if I can find something that will serve for splints. There ought to be something that can be used floating in the water."

"I saw tree branches bobbing about there this afternoon," Harry said, very faintly. "You may be able to find what you want."

Jimmie darted away toward the entrance, and Ned began removing the bandage and the boy's coat and shirtsleeve. His face brightened as he came to understand the extent of the injury.

"I was afraid of a compound fracture," he said, "but this is all right. The flesh is badly swollen, but we'll soon drive that away. Is it very painful?" he continued.

"It hurts like the dickens!" almost sobbed Harry.

"Why didn't the boys fix it?" demanded Ned.

"Because," answered Harry, "someone came to the edge of the pit and called down, and then ran away without giving us any help. We were all afraid he had gone away after some of the half-breeds, and so it seemed that the first thing to do was to get out of sight. After we got in here, they thought they could find their way out by following this tunnel and get to the camp."

In a short time Jimmie returned with several pieces of wood from which splints were made, and then the boy's arm was tenderly cared for.

"There!" Ned exclaimed at the conclusion of the operation, "now you'll be all right in just no time!"

"It's a good thing we're all Boy Scouts, eh?" Jimmie chuckled. "And it's a good thing, too, that one part of the education of a Boy Scout is the care of the injured."

"I never realized before what an advantage it is," Harry said with a faint smile. "I was beginning to think I'd have to remain here all night with the broken bones of that arm grinding together."

"Isn't it about time Jack and Frank were coming back?" asked Ned.

"They should have been here long ago," replied Harry.

"I hope they haven't met with any accident." Jimmie put in. "I'll tell you what I'll do," he went on, "I'll just take a slide down that incline and see if I can dig 'em up anywhere."

"Perhaps you'd better let me go," Ned advised.

"Aw," Jimmie complained, "you always want to cop out all the fun!"

"Well, go on, then," Ned laughed. "If you bump your head against a rock, or get dumped into a pool of water something like the one out there, you mustn't blame me. Remember that I wanted to go."

Jimmie approached the long incline, his electric pointing the way, and soon shouted back:

"This is all right! There's a turn here, and the going is good. Come on in, you fellows. Mighty fine in here!" he went on.

Ned and Harry, the latter now fairly free from pain, made their way slowly to where Jimmie sat hunched up against the side of the wall.

"Cripes!" he exclaimed, "what makes it so wet in here?"

Then Harry explained how the old channel had been cleared of water.

"The boys must have been going some,"

Jimmie put in. ''But look here,'' he went on, ''suppose that old crevice you are talking about should clog or something of that kind? We'd be in a nice mixup down here, wouldn't we?''

"Judging from the noise the water was making in getting out of the pool," Ned suggested, ''I don't think there's much show for the channel clogging. Our only danger from water is that outlaws may dam the present current and flood this channel once more. I don't think there are any outlaws within a mile of us, but still, there's always a chance of their having been summoned by the boy you saw this afternoon.''

''Look here!'' Jimmie observed. ''The boy they saw this afternoon is probably the one who came to the camp and told us where you were. I don't believe he'd bring any outlaws here.''

''Not unless the outlaws desired to bag us all in one bunch,'' Harry added with a smile. ''That may be the idea, you know.''

''My,'' chuckled Jimmie, ''wouldn't Gilroy throw a fit if the outlaws should come and find him sitting there holding the rope? I honestly believe that he'd drop dead with fright.''

''I believe I'll take a walk—or a crawl, rather—out to the mouth of this damp old aqueduct and see what the fat confidential clerk is doing,'' suggested Ned.

''I'll bet you the Michigan Central Railroad

against the Pennsylvania system," Jimmie chuckled, ''that Gilroy has his little old electric lamp trimmed and burning when you get there.''

Ned did not offer to accept the wager, but turned and made his way around the corner and up the long incline. Just as he reached the entrance a cry of terror came to his ears, followed almost immediately by a pistol shot and the fall of a heavy body.

Ned shivered as the unseen form thudded down the awful precipice, bounding, apparently, from one tiny ledge to another, and finally came, with a sickening crash, to the bottom! Only for an instant, however, did it lay on the rocks. There was a splash in the pool and then silence.

Almost shivering with dread, fearing that Gilroy had been shot and hurled from the lip of the cliff, Ned leaned against the wall and waited.

For a time there was no sound at all, and then came a succession of noises which indicated that some one was moving about at the top of the pool so close to the edge that stones dislodged by their feet were bumping down the incline. As the sounds came from two or three directions at once, the boy naturally concluded that the Devil's Punch Bowl was fairly well surrounded. He looked long in the hope of discovering a light or a figure moving dimly against the expanse of stars, but nothing was seen.

The shot had attracted the attention of the boys in the passage, and Jimmie now came panting out to his chum's side.

"What is it?" he asked almost breathlessly.

"There was a shot!" Ned answered. "And some one fell into the pit."

"It must have been Gilroy, then!" Jimmie suggested.

"I'm afraid so," was Ned's anxious reply.

Jimmie listened for a short time and then started away, but Ned drew him back into the shelter of the opening.

"Remain where you are!" he whispered. "There are people moving all around the dip. They may try to come down."

"So that foxy little messenger boy did give us away, did he?" asked Jimmie. "I thought he would all the time!"

"We don't know yet whether he did or not," Ned answered, still in a whisper. "The boy might have been followed when he came here, you know. I can't believe yet that he intentionally led us into danger."

"He always has!" argued Jimmie.

In a moment the rattle of stones was heard again, followed by an exclamation of dismay and a fall. It was such a fall as Ned had heard before—a long, bounding, awful fall, with a sickening crash as of broken flesh and bones at the last!

"Je-rusalem!" whispered Jimmie. "I should think they'd get tired of that after a while."

"I wish I knew where Gilroy is," Ned commented. "I heard him cry out in alarm just before the shot came, then followed the tumble from the top. I'm afraid its all up with Gilroy."

"I should say it was all down with Gilroy if he tipped off that ledge," Jimmie commented.

"Young man," Ned said, "this is too serious a matter to joke about."

"Anyway," Jimmie continued, facetiously, "they wouldn't have to shoot Gilroy to get him rolling down the incline. All they'd have to do would be to poke a finger and yell 'scat!' and away he'd go. Honest, Ned," the boy continued, a little ashamed of his lack of reverence, "that Gilroy is the limit when it comes to getting scared!"

"You must remember," Ned observed, "that this is all new to Gilroy."

"All new!" repeated Jimmie. "I should say so. That fellow doesn't know any more about rough-house than a pig knows about the tariff issue. Actually, Ned, I don't believe he could rough-house a baby cart."

While the boys were talking a faint light appeared at the top of the incline to the east. It wavered about aimlessly for a moment and then passed from view. It was not such a light as would be thrown by an electric torch but rather indicated the flaring of a match in the wind.

Two shots followed the showing of the tiny light, and then a perfect shower of stones rolled down the incline and splashed into the pool at the bottom.

"Gee!" whispered Jimmie. "If I ever get back to little old N. Y., I'm going to have a friend of mine paint this scene for a back-drop in the Devil's auction! Wouldn't it make a hit?"

"Jimmie," Ned reprimanded, "I'd like sometime to see you plunged into a set of circumstances which would throw you into a serious mood."

"Aw, what's the use?" Jimmie returned. "All the wind-jamming I do here won't make any difference with what's going on out there on the pit."

"I'd feel a good deal safer," Ned said in a moment, "if I knew that Frank and Jack were safe. I am beginning to fear that they found an exit through the old passage, and, rather than make their way back up the incline, returned to the pit up the slope."

"I never thought of that," Jimmie answered

very gravely. "Here I've been shooting off hot air at what's going on, and Frank and Jack may be the ones who are getting the kibosh."

As the boy ceased speaking, a bumping, swishing sound was heard, and then footsteps sounded in the pit.

"There!" Jimmie exclaimed. "Some one has come down the rope! Now, who is it? One of the boys, Gilroy or a half-breed?"

## CHAPTER XVII

### A WONDERFUL DISCOVERY

Frank and Jack, when they left Harry near the entrance to the old channel, passed down the incline afterwards followed by their chum and presently came to the turn in the passage. Here they paused for a moment to take note of the situation, and then passed down another incline, much steeper than the other.

"The water must have been going some when it reached this point," Frank suggested. "Put in one straight drop, these tunnels would make Niagara look like thirty cents."

"I wish it had worn a little larger passage," Jack complained, sourly, crawling head foremost into the narrow passage, his flashlight held in advance. "Wouldn't it be fun seeing Gilroy trying to crowd through here," he added. "You could hear him puff for a mile!"

This last steep incline brought the boys to quite a large chamber in the rock. Their lights showed glistening spots in the wall, and they naturally stopped to examine them.

"Gold!" shouted Jack in a moment.

"You bet its gold!" Frank declared. "I

guess I know gold when I see it. Look at it all around us!"

"It is my firm belief," Jack almost shouted, "that we have struck the mother lode! This is the spot where the gold that is washed out in the placers comes from. Don't you think so?"

"It may be," answered Frank, "and I don't wonder that the corporations at war with your father's company are fighting for this hill."

"I don't believe they even know this gold is here," Jack suggested.

"They may not know of this special deposit of gold," Frank continued, "but I'll tell you right now that they do know of a lot of other deposits."

"Yes," Jack returned, "if they didn't know there was gold here in plenty, they wouldn't be putting up such a scrap for the possession of the land. Corporations don't fight for stone piles."

The boys looked over every foot of the chamber, estimating the amount of virgin gold in sight, and almost unconsciously looking for some evidence that the place had been visited before their arrival. Before long Frank stumbled over a slight obstruction on the level floor of the chamber, and almost fell to his knees.

"What the dickens is coming off here?" he shouted.

"Hush!" warned Jack. "What's the use of asking the question of the wide, wide world? We don't know who may be within sound of our voices."

"One thing I do know," Frank grumbled, "and that is that I just about busted my big toe! Now what do you suppose that is?"

He stooped as he spoke and lifted what seemed to be a very crude iron pick from the floor. It was nearly a foot in length, with two sharp points, and in the eye between the two, at the center of the implement, were the remains of a wooden handle, rotted away during long years of disuse. The boys eyed it curiously.

"How's that for a prehistoric implement?" asked Jack.

"It looks as though it might be five thousand years old," Frank answered, taking the implement into his hand.

"It looks to me," Jack declared, "like one of the cave-dweller tools one sees in the Smithsonian Institute at Washington. The scientists declare that such implements were used in the crude mining carried on thousands of years ago. They also state that they were used for beating up Indian corn and refractory wives."

"Anyway," Frank laughed, "the presence of the tool here shows that this chamber was never formed by the action of the water. Those old duffers hewed this out, gathering gold, with just such tools as this."

"And they probably found a good many pounds of gold in every square foot they dug out!" replied Jack.

"Then, look here," Frank said, "if they hewed out this chamber, they built the dam over the old crevice which turned the water into this channel. Can you imagine a better way of concealing millions of dollars worth of gold? I guess they were next to their jobs, all right!"

"I'll tell you what it is," Jack laughed, "when we get back to New York and tell Dad what we've discovered, he ought to buy us a transcontinental railroad apiece. We've earned it all right!"

"Frank looked back toward the narrow incline, and again cast his searchlight over the chamber, which now seemed to them to be a perfect treasure house of virgin gold.

"Did it ever occur to you," he said grimly, "that we've got to get out of this mess before we get back to New York?"

"Yes," Jack replied, "and we've got to make our way out through the continuation of this passage. We couldn't crawl back up that steep passage in a thousand years!"

"And Harry lays back there with a broken arm," Jack added ruefully. "We should have

taken the time to give the boy a little 'first-aid'
before we started out on this excursion. He
must be suffering.''

''Then the thing for us to do now is to keep
plugging along until we get out into God's free
air again. If we can get out ourselves, we can
go back to camp and get a coil of rope and boost
Harry out over the edge of the pit. We never
could get him through this tunnel anyway.''

''That's the ticket!'' Jack answered.

A narrow opening led from the chamber in
which the boys had discovered the gold, and
they followed this for a short distance only to
find themselves confronted by a solid wall of
rock. The tunnel seemed to end there!

''Now,'' questioned Frank, ''how did the
water find its way out of this contraption?
There must be a channel somewhere.''

Jack lowered his electric to the floor of the
passage and then looked up to his chum with
positive fright showing in his face.

''It went plumb down into a hole in the rock!''
he said. ''Here's the hole and it isn't large
enough for a good sized terrier to crawl through.''

''Talk about getting up against the real
thing!'' grumbled Frank.

''Now you just wait a minute,'' Jack suggested. ''There's a current of air here that
doesn't come through the passage by which we

entered.   It blows directly from the north.''

Eagerly the boys turned their lights toward the north wall.

''Here you are!'' Frank shouted in a moment. ''There's another passage here and it's been blocked up with stones!'' The cement with which the stones were sealed has dropped away, and the wind is coming through the cracks. This mine has been worked, all right!''

''What's the matter with pulling the stones down?'' asked Jack.   ''We ought to be able to do that.''

The boys brought all their strength to bear on one of the topmost stones, and it fell with a crash into the passage.

They were about to put their hands to another rock when Jack uttered an exclamation of alarm and drew Frank away.

''This seems to be the haunted mine all right!'' the boy whispered, ''There's a light beyond this wall!''

Frank put his eye to the aperture, gave one look into the interior, and then sprang away.

''It's a wood fire, too!'' he whispered. ''And there are half a dozen as ugly looking gnomes as you ever saw sitting around it.  They must have heard us talking, or heard the stone when it fell, for they are looking this way.  It seems to me,'' he went on, ''that this is one of the quietest little Boy Scout expeditions anyone ever heard of!''

''Shall we try the back passage?'' asked Jack.

''We've got to try it!'' Frank replied. ''At least, we've got to get so far away from this chamber that they won't see us if they come and look through the hole we made in the wall.''

''The danger is,'' Jack decided, ''that they have seen our lights or heard our voices. In that case, here are two Boy Scouts who won't be apt to get out of the tunnel for a few hundred years.''

The heavy tread of footsteps and the sound of guttral voices speaking in a tongue with which the boys were unfamiliar were now heard on the other side of the broken wall, and the boys switched off their lights and started resolutely up the steep grade by means of which they had reached the spot. It was hard climbing and they made slow progress.

While they struggled up the hard slope, after passing the gold chamber, lights flashed in the darkness behind them and they lay flat on their faces, expecting every moment to hear the sounds of determined pursuit.

But the men who had been seen about the fire did not advance beyond the gold chamber. The boys heard them talking together for a moment, and then the sound of their voices died out.

"I guess they've gone back!" ventured Frank.

"I don't believe they have," replied Jack. "Its just this way, you see," he went on, "they would naturally expect to find a current of running water passing through the chamber. Well, we shut the water off, didn't we? That, of itself, will render them suspicious, and they'll keep up their investigation until they find the cause of the change in the stream. I only hope they won't get up to the vicinity of the pit and find Harry before we get back to him!"

Stopping frequently to rest, the boys crawled on up the incline until they came to the angle which led to the first steep passage they had negotiated. By this time, their hands were bleeding from contact with the rough rocks, their breath was coming in short gasps.

Once around the angle, however, they stopped and lay motionless for a moment. Then Frank turned the eye of his searchlight upward. What he saw at the head of the incline caused him to grasp his companion fiercely by the shoulder and point with a trembling finger.

"If that isn't a ghost up there," he said, "it is Harry!"

"We never left Harry as far in the hill as that!" Jack suggested.

"Then its a ghost!" Frank insisted. "Anyway, there's some one up there. I can't see the whole figure, but I saw a white face for just an instant. It must be Harry!"

"Up we go, then!" Jack exclaimed.

The boys were not long kept in doubt as to the identity of the figure they had seen at the top of the incline. Before they had proceeded half a dozen paces, an electric light flashed out, and they saw Harry, evidently startled by the noise of their approach, looking toward them.

"It's Harry, all right!" Jack said. "But that isn't where we left him. He must have crawled down alone."

"Perhaps there's been a mixup on the outside," Frank suggested.

The whispered conversation was interrupted by a soft call from above. The boys recognized the voice of their chum.

"Frank!" Harry whispered.

"All right!" Frank answered.

"Don't make too much noise," Jack suggested. "We've just made the discovery that the heart of this stony old mountain is inhabited."

"Inhabited?" repeated Harry.

"That same!" answered Frank, dropping to the ground at the place where Harry sat. "It's inhabited, and the inhabitants seem to be averse to our efforts as missionaries.''

The boys talked in low tones for a moment before Harry referred to the arrival of Ned and Jimmie. The excitement over the possible pursuit was so great that even this most important event was overlooked!

''Suppose they follow us up here!'' Jack said in a breath. ''We haven't got any more guns than a rabbit!''

''Ned and Jimmie have guns,'' Harry replied.

''Ned and Jimmie?'' repeated both boys.

''Sure!'' answered Harry. ''You scared me so with your talk of mountain gnomes that I forgot to tell you that Ned and Jimmie came into the pit by way of a hempen elevator.''

''Where are they now?'' asked Frank.

''They went out to see what the shooting was about!''

The two boys who had arisen to their feet at mention of their chums' names now dropped flat on the rock.

''I'd like to know what else is coming off here tonight!'' Frank exclaimed. ''There's a herd of cave dwellers chasing us up from behind, and a party of half-breeds trying to shoot us up from in front. Tell you what I'm going to do,'' he went on, ''I'm going to become a disciple of Gilroy. As soon as I get back to little old New York, I'm going to stay there!''

## CHAPTER XVIII

### JIMMIE FINDS A WAY

"That isn't one of the boys," Ned decided as a figure very faintly outlined under the stars approached the place where the two stood.

"Then it must be Gilroy!" Jimmie chuckled. "I guess he got sufficiently frightened to take a trip on our aerial elevator."

"It's Gilroy all right," Ned whispered, in a moment, with a faint suspicion of a chuckle. "And if he hasn't got the rope with him, I'm a goat!"

"I never heard of a man sliding down a rope and bringing the cord with him!" Jimmie laughed. "He must be a wonder!"

Directly the trembling voice of the fat confidential clerk was heard.

"Boys, boys!" he whispered.

"Right here!" Ned answered.

The uncertain figure shot toward the boys as if propelled from the muzzle of a gun. When he reached the spot where they stood, he collapsed utterly and lay groaning on the rocky floor of the entrance to the old channel.

"My God!" he cried. "My God!"

"What's going on up there?" asked Ned.

"Murder!" whimpered the fat clerk. "There's murder going on up there!"

"Who's been killed?" asked Jimmie.

"Oh, I don't know, I don't know!" was the reply. "I sat there holding the rope until I thought you'd deserted me, then I tied it to a point of rock and prepared to descend. Before I could do so, the whole surface of the ledge above the pit became covered with moving figures. They swarmed toward me and I threw myself flat on the ground. I shall never get over the scare I received!"

"Go on," said Ned, impatiently.

"There must have been two parties, or two halves of the same party, coming in from different directions," the confidential clerk continued, "for they fired shots at each other, and I heard one body go tumbling and grinding to the bottom of the pit. It was awful!"

"Then what?" asked Jimmie.

"Then they scuffled about for a time," Gilroy went on, "and I heard more shots and some one else fell. To the end of my life I shall hear the grinding of his bones as he struck the rocks!"

"Did you hear any talk?" asked Ned.

"Oh, I don't know!" was the answer. "I heard talk, but I can't tell you what was said!"

"And then you slid down the rope?" Jimmie asked.

"Yes," was the mournful reply, "and I shall never be able to hold a pen again. My hands are stripped to the bone."

"But how did you manage to bring the rope with you?" asked Ned.

"I can't tell," was the answer. "I think I must have fallen the last few feet, for when I struck the rock the rope came tumbling down on my head. Suppose it had broken away before I reached the bottom," he added with a shudder, "then I should have been lying out there where those other masses of crushed flesh are lying. It was horrible!"

Ned took the cord into his hand and examined it, being careful to step farther into the entrance as he did so, and to turn the light of his electric to the rear.

"The rope was cut!" he said shortly.

"My God!" gasped the fat clerk.

"Cheer up!" Jimmie whispered. "The entertainment has just commenced!"

"Let us get away from this awful place!" pleaded Gilroy.

"I'm agreeable," Jimmie responded. "I'm not stuck on this job myself. Let's go up to the office and get our time!"

"Keep still, you little grouch!" whispered

Ned. "Gilroy is having troubles of his own just now. Don't pester him."

"Oh, well," Jimmie said, "if my cheerful conversation isn't appreciated here, I'll go back and unload some of it on Harry."

"Harry?" repeated Gilroy. "Is he in this nightmare, too?"

"Oh, Harry's all right," Jimmie answered, resolved to get in a parting shot at the frightened man. "Harry's fine as a fiddle. He's got a busted wing, and an annex on his steeple big enough to put a bell in. That's all that's the matter with Harry!"

"Say, Jimmie," Ned interposed, "perhaps you'd better take Gilroy back to the place where we left Harry."

"You come along, too, then!" the boy insisted.

"Perhaps I'd better remain here on the chance of some of the outlaws getting into the pit," Ned suggested.

"According to all accounts, there's two in the pit now," Jimmie chuckled as he turned away. "Now, Gilroy," he continued, taking the frightened man by the arm, "I'll escort you into the chief's office, and give you the third degree! I think you'll learn to like this place!"

The two disappeared in the darkness, Jimmie wisely restraining an inclination to light the way

with his electric.    Ned remained at the entrance
for some moments, listening for further evidences
of an attack, but none came.    Then he heard
footsteps and heard a chuckle close behind.

"What do you think?" Jimmie asked. "Jack
and Frank have crawled out of the bottomless
pit and are back there trying to comfort Harry.
As for Gilroy, he's trying to send his sobs by
wireless to New York."

"What's the use tantalizing Gilroy!" Ned
said, unable to restrain a laugh.    "You've got
him so scared now that he doesn't know
which way is from him.    Why don't you let him
alone?"

"I try to let him alone." Jimmie replied with
assumed gravity, "but when I think how fat he
is, and how his face reminds me of a cold roast
of veal, I just can't help stirring him up a bit."

"So Jack and Frank didn't succeed in finding
a route out by the dry channel?" asked Ned.

"I guess not," Jimmie replied.    "I didn't
stop to ask many questions, for I wanted to let
you know that they were here."

"I think," Ned said after a moment's silence,
"that the war is over for tonight.    There isn't
a whisper at the top of the cliff now."

In order to make sure that the outlaws had
indeed departed, Ned and Jimmie stood for some

moments in the entrance just beyond the angle of the wall.

While they stood there a mellow mist of light filled the sky, revealing the sharp outlines of the ledge at the top of the pit.

"Perhaps they're building a fire," suggested Jimmie.

"The moon!" replied Ned.

"I'm mighty glad to see her!" Jimmie responded.

Ned looked at his watch under the hidden ray of a searchlight and went on:

"Eleven o'clock," he said.   "The moon must have been in view for some minutes."

"Of course," Jimmie answered.   "It wouldn't be shining on the western slope of this blooming old dump if it hadn't."

"In half an hour or so, then," Ned said, "we may be able to learn whether the outlaws have indeed taken their departure."

"You go on in and see Frank and Jack," Jimmie suggested, "and take the rope with you. They want to tell you something they've discovered.   They wouldn't tell me, but I'm positive that they've blundered on a deposit of gold.   They look happy enough to have found a million."

"I hope they haven't said anything about it to Gilroy," Ned replied.

"Gilroy?" repeated Jimmie scornfully. "Why that fat dub is scared stiff. He wouldn't know the Constitution of the United States from a declaration of war right now."

"Don't go to getting into any scrapes while I'm gone," Ned advised, as he turned away toward the tunnel. "You stand right here and keep watch until I come back."

"I won't breathe aloud!" promised Jimmie.

The meeting between Ned and the other boys was a joyous one. Each had been worried over the disappearance of the other. As for Gilroy, he welcomed the assembling of the boys as an indication that he was soon to be taken out of the dangerous situation in which he found himself.

"Now, boys," Ned said, after the greetings were over, "we've got to get Harry up the incline and out of the pit, so we may as well be at it."

"According to Gilroy," Harry smiled, "there's a band of Bashi Bazooks up there ready to mix with you the minute you show your faces."

"The killing of two of their number undoubtedly frightened them away," Ned answered. "At any rate the moon is rising now, and any danger which threatens may readily be detected. You must understand," he went on, "that the outlaws who came to the Devil's

Punch Bowl expected to find you three boys lying dead at the bottom."

"Why should they think that?" asked Harry.

"I'm going on the theory," replied Ned, "that this crooked little messenger boy notified the outlaws where we were to be found before he came to lead us to the slaughter."

"That's just about what he did!" Jack interposed.

"In that case," Ned continued, "When they saw no trace of us in the pit, they were ready to abandon their search, probably believing that the boy had deceived them."

"I understand," Frank cut in, "then they got into a mixup among themselves and, according to Gilroy, two were killed and the rest took a hot-foot for the cool chambers of the old mission."

"That's the way I look at it," Ned said.

"Then we may as well be getting Harry out," Frank suggested. "We'll tie the rope under his arms, use our coats for a stretcher and pull him gently, yet firmly, up the tunnel until his back wears out and then we'll turn him over."

"I could walk up all right," Harry insisted, "if the tunnel was only high enough for me to stand up in."

"But it isn't," Jack returned. "We've all got to crawl on our hands and knees, and you never can do it with that bum wing of yours."

"No," Frank advised, "you never can climb up the tunnel with a broken arm. We'll bundle you up in our coats, tie you tight like a mummy with the rope, and then pull you up. The floor of the tunnel is so smooth that you'll think you're out sleigh-riding on a winter night."

This plan was followed, and the injured boy was landed at the entrance of the old channel with very little inconvenience.

The moon was higher in the heavens now, and its light illuminated not only the circle of jagged rocks which held the pit in their setting but also a portion of the depression itself. Ned searched the top with a field glass but found no evidence of enemies.

"The way is clear, I think," he decided, "and the question now before the house is as to how we're going to get that rope up."

"Don't be asking foolish questions," Jimmie cut in. "Frank and Jack wormed their way down here, didn't they?"

"Indeed we did," Jack answered, "and came very near breaking our necks half a dozen times!"

"Then I can worm my way up!" Jimmie insisted. "Here," he went on, "you see that crooked corner of rock twenty or thirty feet up? Well, just throw the rope over that and I'll get up that far anyway. I think I can see resting places for the rope at intervals all the way up. I'm the original aerial climber!"

"We don't want another boy with broken limbs," suggested Frank.

"If I get a tumble," Jimmie advised, "you won't have any trouble picking me up. You can carry me home in your pockets."

The mode of climbing the precipice suggested by the lad was not so difficult as it at first appeared to be. With the aid of the rope, a strong arm, and infinite daring, the boy soon reached the lip of the pit and the rest was easy. when all were at the top, Jimmie reminded his companions that they had paid no attention to the bodies of the two men who had fallen over the precipice.

In spite of the protests of the others, the little fellow insisted on swinging down the rope, now stretching from top to bottom, and making a search for the two bodies. When he returned to the top, his face was a little paler than usual, and he started away without a word.

"Who are they?" asked Ned, provoked at the boy's silence.

"One of them is the man called Huga by the fellows in the old mission cave," he answered, "and the other is just a common mucker."

"With Huga dead," Ned said, "the way is easier."

## CHAPTER XIX

### A BOY SCOUT ENCOUNTER

When the boys started back over the long and difficult route to the camp, the moon was shining brightly on the mountains. There were no indications of strife anywhere. There were no sounds to break the stillness save those made by the boys in their passage over the loose rocks.

They had proceeded only a short distance when Jimmie darted away from the group and disappeared behind a crag which jutted out to the west. Ned and the others stopped in their tracks and looked about in wonder and perplexity.

"What's that little monkey up to now?" asked Frank rather impatiently.

"He may be trying to get a rabbit for breakfast," Jack replied with a grin. "We haven't had anything to eat for a long time, you know, and I presume that Jimmie is about ready to make a meal out of granite."

"Well," Ned said in a moment, "we'll go right on and leave the little rascal to his own devices. If he gets a squirrel for breakfast, we'll help him eat it, and that's the best we can do!"

The boys had proceeded but a short distance when a sound which startled them as no other could have done at that particular time reached their ears. It was the high, quavering, vicious call of the wolf pack!

The boys paused again and scattered, each one taking a few steps away from the common center. As for Gilroy, he squatted flat on the ground and covered his fat face with trembling fingers.

"Wolves!" he cried. "Oh, my God, wolves!"

While feeling sympathy for the man lacking entirely in physical courage, Ned could not restrain a burst of laughter.

"Is that Jimmie?" Jack asked in a moment.

"I should say not!" answered Frank. "Jimmie hasn't got a tenor voice to that extent. That's not Jimmie!"

"Then it's that treacherous rat of a messenger boy!" Harry declared.

"Answer him, some one!" Frank advised, "and we'll get our hands on him." It was not necessary for one of the group to answer the call, for in a moment, almost like an echo, the answer came from behind the boulder where Jimmie had secreted himself.

"That's Jimmie!" cried Frank. "Now do

you suppose that little rat saw Norman before we heard the call?"

"It seems that he did," answered Ned. "Jimmie rather favored the boy at first but now there'll be a mixup if they meet."

"Then I hope they'll meet," grumbled Frank. "Just look at the trouble that boy has made for us since we've been here. He'll get his!"

Seeing the boys standing so unconcerned and talking so coolly, Gilroy looked up with a little less alarm showing in his face, and finally arose to his feet. His knees were trembling so that they almost bent under him.

"Did you hear it?" he asked in a shaking voice. "Did you hear the wolf calling to his mates? There'll be a pack here directly. I know, because I had an experience with wolves when I was sent into the Dakotas on business by Mr. Bosworth. Why don't you boys do something?"

"That was the call of the the wolf pack all right!" Frank exclaimed. "But the wolves it summed were only Boy Scouts of the Wolf Patrol."

Gilroy seemed overjoyed at the information, and even ventured on toward the rock from which the last call had proceeded.

"I'd like to know why that little monkey of

a Jimmie doesn't show up?" asked Jack in a moment. "He ought to be here now."

At this moment a great threshing and puffing came from the rear of the rock, and the boys rushed in that direction. What they saw caused them to dance with excitement and repeat the call of the pack until the mountains rang again.

Jimmie and Norman were having it out on a level space behind the rock! They were not doing each other any serious harm, but they were rolling and tumbling about, locked in each other's arms, at a great rate. As Ned drew near, Jimmie gained a decided advantage, and in a moment was calmly sitting on Norman's stomach wiping the perspiration from his face.

"Wolves trying to eat each other!" laughed Jack.

"Huh!" stormed Jimmie, "this ain't no wolf. This is only a dirty dog that sneaked into the pack. I'm going to give him what's coming to him! He deserves a good beating up for what he has done to us!"

"Pry him loose!" shouted Norman, half laughing at the predicament in which he had been discovered, "and I'll tell you all about it."

"Yes you will!" shouted Jimmie. "You'll tell us another pack of lies and get us into more trouble. Why," he went on, "I wouldn't believe you if you said that round thing up there in the sky is the moon."

"Get up," Ned advised, "and give the boy a chance."

Jimmie arose, reluctantly, and Norman soon got to his feet.

"I said I'd tell you all about it some day," Norman began, "and I'm going to do it right now!"

"Don't work your imagination overtime!" scoffed Jimmie.

"Go on!" Ned suggested. "Say what you have to say. But let me tell you this," he went on, "your story will have to be pretty straight, and not include any excursions into the land of the enemy, in order to be believed. You must remember that we've had trouble following your steers."

"Don't you believe a word he says!" almost shouted Gilroy, thinking only of his own inconvenience. "It was his fault that I was led to that awful Devil's Punch Bowl. I'll never get over that experience as long as I live! It was horrible—beyond belief."

"Go on, Norman," Ned advised. "Make it short!"

"I told you once," the boy began, "that something terrible would happen to a person in New York if I ever gave Toombs any cause to believe that I wasn't perfectly loyal to his interests."

"I remember that," Ned answered. "Go on!"

"That person," Norman continued, "is my sister, a pretty girl of eighteen—though you wouldn't believe she could be pretty, being my sister—who became employed in Toombs' Wall street office a year ago. We lived together upon East Tenth street, and both had to work. When she secured the place in Toombs' office we thought our fortunes were made, and for a time everything went well."

"Aw, cut it short!" Jimmie hinted. "We don't believe a word of it, you know, so you may as well ring off right now."

"Don't interrupt the boy," Ned suggested. "Let him tell his story in his own way. We have plenty of time."

"One day," Norman continued," a large sum of money—something like five thousand dollars—very mysteriously disappeared from Toombs' safe. At least Toombs declared the money had been taken. Some of us never believed the story he told.

"The only person having a knowledge of the combination of the safe except Toombs himself was my sister. She was accused of taking the money, and Toombs threatened prosecution. At last he promised not to turn the matter over

to the police if we would both promise to return
the money."

"Gee!" declared Jimmie in a friendlier tone.
"That was a life sentence all right, wasn't it?
I don't believe he ever lost any money."

"We have been paying that old thief a portion
of our wages ever since," Norman went on.
"Then, a few weeks ago, when he promised to
square the whole account if I would do certain
work for him in connection with the Wolf
Patrol, I was forced to consent. He threatened
that if I did not consent he would set the law in
motion and send my sister to prison."

"What did he want you to do in connection
with the Wolf Patrol?" demanded Ned. "I
don't understand how you could help him
through the Patrol. Wall street knows little
of Boy Scouts."

"When you boys reached San Francisco, after
your bout with the train robbers," Norman
answered, "the newspaper owned by Frank's
father printed a long story about the Boy
Electricians. At the end of the article was a
statement to the effect that the boys were going
into camp near Twin Peaks. Now, this is the
point toward which Toombs' activities had been
directed for a long time."

"I know that," answered Ned. "He is trying

to rob corporations represented by Jack's father of their property."

"I don't know why," the boy went on, "but he has been paying a great deal of attention to this section for a long time. He has had detectives here rounding up half-breeds, and has been hunting high and low in all the abstract offices of the west for papers which he claims are wrongfully withheld from him. There seems to be a great deal at stake."

"You bet there is," laughed Jack, nudging Frank. "There is more at stake than that old slob knows anything about."

"When Toombs saw that Lawyer Bosworth's son was headed for this part of the country, accompanied by Ned Nestor, well known over the world as a very successful juvenile detective, he just ran around in circles, he was so excited about it. It was then that he proposed to me to come on here with him, ostensibly as a cook in his camp, but really as a spy, and learn what you boys were up to. I had to come. What else could I do?

"There was my sister in New York, waiting for me to wipe out the unlawful indebtedness, and I couldn't disappoint her. He could have thrown her into the Tombs prison with ten words sent by wire."

"That's a pretty rotten proposition, isn't it?" demanded Jimmie.

"Rotten is no name for it!" agreed Jack.

"Toombs and his gang of mercenaries arrived in the vicinity of the old Franciscan mission long before you boys came into the mountains. I was with him, of course, acting as cook, and for a few days I enjoyed myself hugely. Then you boys came in, and I was ordered to deliver that note to Ned. But before the morning I saw you boys in camp and delivered the note, I had seen you all in your beds.

"Because of some trivial disobedience of orders, Toombs had decreed that I should go supperless to bed. What I did, I think, was to scorch his steak. Anyway, he said, that I shouldn't have anything to eat until the next day at noon."

"No wonder you grabbed for our grub closet!" laughed Jimmie.

"I was good and hungry that night all right," Norman answered with a smile. "But I didn't eat all the stuff I took away. I hid it in the forest so as to be provided with food when I finally gained the courage to beat Toombs over the head with a club and escape."

"Did you really think of doing that?" chuckled Jimmie.

"I thought of doing it," was the answer, "but

I don't know whether I should ever have acquired the courage. There was my sister waiting in New York, you know. Anyway, I hid
the beans and part of the bread not far away
from your camp."

"Why didn't you wake us up?" asked Ned.

"I wanted to," was the reply, "but I didn't
know what to do. I was afraid you would in
some way let Toombs understand that I was
playing into your hands. I didn't think you
would betray me knowingly, but I thought that
some careless act on your part might send my
sister to prison."

"I can't blame you for being cautious," Ned
answered.

"The next morning, when we saw the two
in the pine woods, that is, when Toombs and I
came upon them there, Toombs laid the plot to
get Ned into his hands by sending the note which
I afterwards delivered. You must remember
that I tried to warn you at that time, boys," he
added.

"Yes, you told us to beat it!" Frank said.

"After that," Norman continued, "I gave
the Indian smoke signal in order to confirm you
in the belief that I really was a Boy Scout in
good standing. I didn't know then that Jimmie
would start off alone to investigate and get
cornered by the half-breeds. I didn't know,

either," he added, "that the half-breeds were so thick about the place where Frank and the others were captured.

"And when I warned you," he added, turning to Ned, "that the boys were in a bad fix in the Devil's Punch Bowl, I did it in good faith. I have since learned that I was followed last night, and that the half-breed who came after me saw the boys in the pit and went back after the gang.

"Huga, Toombs' right-hand man, was killed at the pit, and the old man is wild with anger. He can't control the half-breeds without Huga. They have already deserted him. In fact, there is only one person with him at the old mission now, and that is a Hoola Indian named Sigma. This Indian is one of the descendants of the tribe of Indians which long claimed this property as their own under a grant from the Mexican government. He is said to know more about the mountains hereabouts than any other living person."

"Is he a real Hoola Indian?" asked Frank, rather anxiously.

"He is said to be," answered Norman.

"Are there other Hoolas about?" demanded Jack.

"A few have been seen—perhaps less than a dozen."

"Then if there really should be an extensive deposit of gold in this section," Frank asked, "this Sigma might know something about it?"

"He would know about it if any one did."

Frank beckoned Ned and Jack to one side where they could talk without being overheard by the others. Then Frank very briefly explained the discovery of the gold chamber and added:

"If this Hoola Indian knows all about the deposit of gold, he'll tell Toombs, and the New York bunch will get possession of it in some way. Now, what are we going to do?"

"Perhaps we'd better hear Norman out first," Ned said, after expressing surprise that such a store of gold should remain so long undiscovered by the seekers after the precious metal. "Norman may know something more concerning this Indian."

"Where do these Indians make their headquarters?" Ned asked, returning to the others.

"No one knows," Norman answered. "They come and go like ghosts. It is common talk that they know where great deposits of gold are located but no one has ever been able to follow them to their store-house. They always have plenty of virgin gold, and are very independent."

"Have you ever tried following this Sigma?" asked Ned.

"I followed him one moonlight night,"
Norman replied. "He climbed the cliff which
faces the east and backs against the Devil's
Punch Bowl. He made his way almost to the
summit, and there disappeared. I searched the
locality thoroughly, but all I discovered was a
great smooth space of rock overlooking the east.
Carved in deep lines upon this rock where the
outlines of the flag of Spain, crown and all! I
don't think anyone ever saw it before—anyone
save the Indians. After discovering it, however, I found no difficulty in tracing it out from
the valley."

## CHAPTER XX

### THE FLAG ON THE CLIFF

"And the flag on the cliff indicates the spot where the gold was stored by nature long ago!" Frank whispered to Ned.

"I beg your pardon, boys," suggested Gilroy stepping forward to where Ned and Frank were standing, "but if you'll kindly direct me toward the camp, I'll manage to get on alone. The fact of the matter is," he continued, "that I'm faint with hunger."

"Faint with hunger!" echoed Jimmie. "Mother of Moses! If you were half as hungry as I am, you'd be eating rock. I haven't had anything to eat in so long that I wouldn't know whether to chew a bear steak or to drink it. I'm near dead right now."

"I think we'd all better hurry back to camp," Ned suggested. "We may find something of a mixup there."

"May I go with you?" asked Norman humbly.

"What about Toombs?" asked Ned. "If you are seen in our company, the telegram you have good reason to fear may be sent on to New York as soon as he can get out of the wilderness."

Norman turned paler under the light of the moon and shrank back as if from a blow. His voice trembled as he spoke.

"I thank you for reminding me of my duty to my sister," he said. "I'm afraid I'll have to go back to Toombs. I don't know what he'll do to me because of my long absence, and because of the suspicious circumstances under which I left the camp. I'm afraid of him!"

"Now look here, Norman," Frank advised, "this man Toombs is a welcher. He's a dirty cur, and never kept a promise in his life which it was to his interest to disregard. Whatever you do for him, he'll exact the last cent of the obligation which he has placed upon you, and will then, at the slightest whim, turn your sister over to the law. I don't want to give you any advice calculated to get you into trouble, but were I in your place I think I'd go back there and beat his head off! The more you do for him, the stronger will be his grip upon you."

"And I regard that as good advice!" Jack declared.

"Very good!" Nestor commented.

"I'll go back with you if you want to beat him up!" offered Jimmie.

"And I'll go along, too," Harry said. "I've

got a bum arm, all right, but I think I could help push that fellow into the Devil's Punch Bowl."

"Don't resort to violence, boys! Don't resort to violence!" pleaded Gilroy. "I'm shocked now to think how the laws of our country have been disobeyed tonight. Don't go back to get into more trouble!"

"But look here," exclaimed Jimmie, "you don't know how smooth and fat and vicious this man Toombs is. I have never seen much of him, but I'll tell you right now that he breathes out an atmosphere like that of a snake. I'll get his goat yet!"

"Don't be putting wild notions into the boy's head," laughed Frank. "I've got a better way than that to round up the old sea-serpent. We can get a messenger out to the telegraph station just as quickly as he can—perhaps quicker if we set Gilroy on the trail tonight. Now, I'll write a long message to Dad and tell him all about it, and Dad's got a pull in New York."

"He'll go to the District Attorney and calmly announce that he'll smash him all to little pieces in his newspaper if he causes the arrest of that girl until after a full investigation has been made. What Dad can do in the District Attorney's office is a wonder! We'll fix old

Toombs all right, all right! We'll have him in jail as soon as he gets back to New York!"

"Will you start off toward the nearest telegraph office tonight, Gilroy?" asked Ned. "This is important, you know."

"Give me something to eat and let me sleep a couple of hours," replied the fat clerk, "and I'll gladly go! I wouldn't stay in this country one more day for all the gold there is in it!"'

"Well, then," Jack cut in, "I'll send a telegram to my Dad, and he'll co-operate with Frank's ancestor, and I guess they can arrange matters so the girl won't be arrested. If Dad isn't in New York when the wire arrives, his confidential clerk will attend to it. I have them all trained to jump when I say the word. Dad lets me do just as I please, and they have to follow his example."

"Now, Norman," Ned exclaimed, "you may as well give Toombs the hook and come on back to camp with us. These two boys can do more for you in New York than a host of lawyers and bondsmen could do in a hundred years."

"That's good sense!" Harry exclaimed. "Come on back to camp with us and we'll fat you up!"

"I'm going to assault the next person that talks about eating!" Jimmie declared. "Here I'm half starved to death and you keep on talking about eating. If you fellows had any pity in your hearts, some of you would run on ahead and meet me at the camp with a pie!"

"Well," Frank said in a moment, "I don't know why we don't all hurry back to the camp. We may as well talk there as here. It's all right to stroll and talk in the moonlight, but I never could be romantic when I was hungry. It's agin' human nature!"

The boys made good progress for an hour or more, and just as day was breaking, they came within sight of the cliff under which their camp was situated. They stood looking down from a higher elevation for a moment and then Ned pointed away to the south and east.

"Listen!" he said, bending his head forward.

"Bells!" shouted Jimmie. "Bells ringing at this time of the morning, away up in the Sierra Nevada Mountains! What do you make of that?"

"Mule bells!" scoffed Jimmie.

"I guess that's right," Harry agreed. "And there are the mules," he went on, pointing. "They've brought some one in!"

"If they would only stop long enough to take me out!" wailed Gilroy, starting off as if in pursuit of the distant train of mules.

"Those beasts of burden are two hours' travel from this point," Frank advised. "They look to be only a short distance off, but you'd have to climb over a whole lot of land standing up on end to get to them."

"Now who do you think the latest arrival is?" asked Jimmie.

"Probably a message from Dad," Jack suggested.

"I'm sure of that!" Gilroy cried, gleefully. "I'm sure its an order for my recall. I'll soon be out of this terrible country, safe in little old New York! It's too good to be true!"

The boys now hastened toward the cliff and, turning sharply around the angle of rock, saw that the camp had indeed been occupied since their departure. A fire, which gave every indication of having recently been built, was burning and a number of cooking utensils stood near by.

Jimmie was about to spring forward for the purpose of making an assault on the provision chest when Ned caught him by the arm and held him back. Jimmie scowled by remained silent.

"Listen!" Ned said in a very low whisper. "There are people talking in the cave! I propose to find out what's going on before making my appearance. Get the boys farther away," he went on, "and I'll see what I can learn. We may not be out of trouble yet."

"Why, that's the person that came in with the mule train," whispered Jimmie. "Anyone ought to know that!"

"I don't know whether it is or not!" Ned insisted. "Get the boys away and keep still, all of you."

Gilroy opened his mouth to protest against being separated from the supply of food so near at hand, but Jimmie clapped a hand over his lips and led him away by main force. Then Ned crouched under the stones of the barrier and listened.

"It's all up with you, Bosworth!" he heard the voice of Toombs saying. "You played your last card when you came in here in person, and I've taken the trick! Now you may as well be good!"

"No game is ever played out until the last card is on the table!" Jack's father was heard to say. "You said when you came in here," the lawyer went on, "that you would give me information of my son."

"All in good time!" replied Toombs. "I understand," the Wall street man continued "that you have in your possession papers showing the location of a very valuable mine known to exist in this section hundreds of years ago. Inform me as to the location of this mine, and I'll inform you fully regarding your son."

"Toombs," Bosworth replied, "I wouldn't trust you with a dirty bone that a dog wouldn't take from my hand. You're one of the pirates of Wall street! You never earned an honest dollar in your life. There are murders which might be laid at your door. You have wrecked private fortunes, and are no more to be trusted than a deadly rattler!"

Ned chuckled at this arraignment of the man who had given him so much trouble. The conversation certainly was amusing to him.

"Hard words break no bones!" laughed Toombs. "Say what you please, only give me the information I demand. And I insist on something more than the information, too," he went on. "I want your promise that the corporation you represent will quit-claim all these lands to me."

"To you?" asked Bosworth scornfully.

"Yes, to me!"

"Not to your clients, but to you personally?"

"To me, personally!"

Thus placing you in a position to rob and blackmail your employers?"

"Call it what you like," Toombs answered.

"I had been giving you credit for loyalty to the members of your theiving gang," Bosworth said. "I see that I was mistaken."

"But the information?" demanded Toombs.

"There are no such documents as you describe in existence!" the lawyer answered. "If there are, I am ignorant of the fact."

Ned heard some one moving about in the cave, and then Toombs' voice came again, speaking harshly and with vicious rage.

"You may as well accompany me to my camp," Toombs said. "We can settle matters better there!"

"I shall not leave this place!" was the calm reply.

"But why wait longer here?" Toombs demanded fiercely. "This is a deserted camp. The boys who occupied it yesterday are dead, drowned at the Devil's Punch Bowl. Your son with the others. You have no one in the hills to whom you can appeal for aid. If you persist in your refusal to deliver the papers and the information, you shall share the same fate. Will you come quietly?"

There was a scuffle and a blow, and when Ned gained the interior of the cave, he saw Bosworth lying on the floor with the blood springing from a slight wound on the forehead. Toombs made a motion toward his pistol-pocket as Ned appeared, but he was too late. A blow from the butt of the boy's weapon laid him on the ground beside his victim.

Then the boys all came rushing in, and Jack

was with difficulty restrained from giving the half-conscious Toombs a very bad beating.

"Let him alone," Ned advised. "We'll tie him up and take him out with us. There are many charges which can be placed against him."

Jack's father soon regained consciousness, and there followed a long and intimate conversation between the two. Too anxious to remain in New York after the departure of Gilroy, the father had followed on, trying his best to reach Gilroy by wire, but failing. He had traveled night and day, reaching the camp only three hours before the arrival of the boys.

The reader may well understand the kind of a meal that was prepared just after sunrise. After even Jimmie was satisfied the boys went to sleep, leaving Gilroy, who declared that he could never sleep again, moving about the camp. After a couple of hours the boys were awakened by shrill screams issuing from the throat of the fat clerk.

"The Indians! The Indians!" he shouted.

Ned sprang to his feet and looked keenly about but at first saw no cause for alarm. What he did see in a moment, however, brought a flush of anger to his face. The place where Toombs had lain was unoccupied! In some mysterious manner, the fellow had made his escape while the boys slept!

"The Indians did it!" insisted Gilroy, his teeth chattering with fright. "I saw an Indian creep up and cut the ropes. I was so frozen of terror that I couldn't stop him. An awful, painted savage! He threatened me with a knife when I managed to look in his direction."

While Gilroy was making this explanation, Jimmie sprang to his feet and darted swiftly out of the cave. Ned called to him to return, but he paid no attention. In a moment the boy was out of sight.

## CHAPTER XXI

### THE END OF A CROOKED ROAD

Leaving the boys in wild commotion at the camp, Jimmie followed swiftly on in the direction which he believed Toombs to have taken.

"I just can't let that geezer get away!" the boy muttered as he traveled over the rough ground at great speed.

After half an hour's steady walking he came to an elevation from which he saw two figures moving away to the north. One of the men seemed to him to be Toombs, while the other might well be classed as an Indian. They were moving at a good pace, although the Indian was frequently obliged to assist his companion over rocky crags.

The two seemed entirely unconscious of pursuit. Indeed, as it was afterwards learned, they were beyond the sound of Gilroy's voice when he shouted out the alarm which had awakened the boys. The fat clerk had been so frightened that he had made no attempt to sound an alarm until the Indian he feared was too far away to inflict injury upon him!

And so, believing that the boys still slept in

the camp, and that the escape of their prisoner still remained undiscovered, the two made their way, not to the old camp near the mission, but toward the sheltered bit of ground which enclosed the Devil's Punch Bowl.

"Now, I wonder why they are going there!" mused Jimmie, gaining upon the two fugitives every moment. "If that fellow who cut Toombs out of our camp," he went on, "should prove to be a Hoola Indian, fully advised as to the deposit of gold, he might give Toombs information calculated to make us a lot of trouble."

The boy was satisfied that neither Toombs nor any of the half-breeds possessed any information concerning the hidden mine. According to Norman's story, only the Hoola Indians knew about the wonderful deposit which the boys had blundered upon during their trip to the underground passage. His thought now was that the Indian with Toombs might be leading that individual to the treasure.

Wishing earnestly that he had not started on such a mission alone, the boy followed on until the two stopped at the very verge of the Devil's Punch Bowl. By this time Jimmie was completely exhausted. He had been on his feet all night, laboring under great excitement, and had had only a short bit of rest after breakfast. He was, therefore, more than glad when

Toombs and the Indian paused at the Devil's Punch Bowl and threw themselves on the ground.

Lying behind a boulder, the boy saw the Indian pointing down into the pit, and it seemed to him that he was directing the attention of his companion to the old channel where he, Jimmie, had met with such exciting adventures.

"It's dollars to doughnuts," the boy mused, "that that's Sigma, the Indian, Norman referred to. If it is, he's showing Toombs where the gold mine is. That's just our luck, anyway!"

Foot by foot the boy passed from one rock to another until he came within sound of the men's voices. He could not understand what the Indian was saying, but Toombs seemed to be able to grasp the meaning of the uncouth words used.

"And you say there are tons of gold under there?" the boy heard Toombs ask. "Is there any way of getting at it at once?"

Jimmie saw Sigma nod his head vigorously.

"Can you understand exactly what I say?" Toombs asked in a moment.

Sigma nodded again, and the Wall street man went on:

"What we want to do right now," he said,

"is to get the gold out without any publicity whatever. Do you understand that?"

The Indian looked puzzled at the long words used, but nodded. It was evident that he understood the general import of the other's talk.

"The men I represent," Toombs went on, "would throw a few dirty dollars into my lap for information which would bring them millions. Now my idea is to get the gold out and get away with it."

"Say, Toombs," Jimmie whispered to himself behind the rock, "you're a dirty old schemer!"

"With the gold in our possession, we can disappear from the country, you and I. We need never trouble ourselves about money any more."

The Indian nodded while a pleased smile came over his rugged face.

"How many know of this mine?" asked Toombs.

Sigma held up eight fingers and pointed into the pit.

"Only that many?" asked Toombs.

"The rest dead!" answered Sigma.

"And where are they now?" demanded the Wall street man.

"All in the mine getting out gold!" was the reply.

"They can get it out pretty fast, can't they?" asked Toombs.

The Indian nodded, and said in a guttural voice that many great heaps of it had already been taken out of the rock and stored in the inner chamber. Toombs' eyes brightened wickedly at the information.

"And they're all in there now?" he asked. "All the heaps?"

Sigma nodded again.

"We don't want anyone watching us," Toombs explained, "so we must make sure about their all being in the cave. You go through the dry channel and find out if they are all really there, then come to the entrance and signal to me and go back and explain what we have planned—that I am to market the gold, for them and receive half."

"Now it strikes me," Jimmie mused, "that if I were in Sigma's place, I wouldn't go into that old channel and leave Toombs on the outside, especially if every living person having knowledge of the deposit of gold was on the inside, too!"

The Indian disappeared over the edge of the Devil's Punch Bowl and made his way to the bottom, pursuing practically the same tactics resorted to by the boys the day before. As soon as he disappeared in the old dry channel,

Toombs, who had carefully watched the Indian's every move, proceeded to follow into the depression.

The man was fat, unwieldy, and out of training, but his greed for gold was so great, his daring so remarkable, that he managed to reach the bottom of the pit with only a few slight bruises. Jimmie lay down at the lip of the pit and regarded him quizzically.

"I'd like to know what the game is," the boy thought.

The tragedy enacted before his eyes during the next hour informed him fully on this point.

In a short time Sigma returned to the entrance of the old channel and held up eight fingers to Toombs. His face showed surprise at seeing the Wall street man at the bottom of the pit. After giving the signal he stood with his head bowed for a moment, as if in deep thought, and then turned back into the tunnel.

It was then that the real purpose of the Wall street man became known. He threw off his coat and vest and began filling the channel leading to the crevice, now carrying away the waters of the pool! He worked frantically until the sweat streamed down his face in tiny rivulets. notwithstanding the cool air of the mountain.

At first he dug away with his fingers, but that appeared to be too slow a process for his eager haste. There were pieces of shale lying about which the boys had used the previous afternoon, and with these he made much better progress.

Although it had taken the boys a long time to dig the trench connecting the pool with its original outlet, it was by no means difficult for Toombs to fill in the channel in a very short time. Slowly but steadily the waters of the pool lifted as the obstructions in its channel forced the water toward the level of the old outlet.

While the man worked nervously, strenuously, and with such strength as he would never have been able to exhibit at ordinary times, Jimmie saw the dark face of Sigma appear at the opening. The Indian stood for an instant with folded hands as he saw what Toombs was doing.

"It's all up with the fat Wall street man now!" Jimmie mused. "The Indians are wise to the fact that his only purpose in sending Sigma in was to bunch those possessing information of the mine and drown them all like a lot of baby cats. What they'll do to him now will be a plenty. I wouldn't be in his shoes for a good deal."

So busily was Toombs engaged in his work that he did not hear the smothered ejaculations or the soft footsteps of the Indian as he crept up behind him. It was evident that he believed the Indians to be all massed in the gold chamber.

When, at last, he was seized in the muscular grasp of the Indian, the boy saw him smile, evidently trying to explain away his actions. Sigma shook his head and uttered a peculiar cry. The next moment seven Indians came from the entrance and gathered around the now crestfallen Wall street man.

There was not much talk. In fact, Jimmie could not hear a word that was spoken. All he knew was that there was no delay. The Indians took up the work of filling the channel which Toombs had begun. Then, when it was quite full and the water was roaring and swirling into the entrance so recently vacated, they bound Toombs hand and foot and cast him into the torrent.

Jimmie gave a low groan of horror and turned away. He knew that Toombs fully deserved his fate. Still, his punishment seemed to be a brutal one. He knew that the mangled body of the unfortunate man would be swept from level to level and from rock to rock until it came to the round aperture in the floor which carried the water straight down for how many hundred feet no one could estimate.

He knew that in time the Indians would find a way of getting out the gold unless the corporation represented by Jack's father should take advantage of the information secured by the

Boy Scouts and get the gold in advance. He knew, too, that Toombs' craving for gold would at last be satisfied. For a long time his body would swing about in eddys which whirled about heaps of gold worthy a king's ransom.

"Serves him just right!" the boy mused as he turned away. "He was the crookedest man that ever lived. And now," he added with a sigh, "I'll get back to camp and see if the boys have been cooking anything more to eat."

When he reached the camp, a great kettle of bear stew was simmering over the fire, and Frank and Jack were explaining to Mr. Bosworth the story of the night and telling of the discovery of the wonderful deposit of gold in the vicinity of the Devil's Punch Bowl. The capitalist seemed overjoyed at the success of the expedition, and when Jimmie, in a voice not very strong, described the death of Toombs and the re-flooding of the mine, the silence was broken only by exclamations of pity for the man whose greed had led him to such a frightful death.

"But how are we going to get this gold out, now that the mine is flooded?" asked Mr. Bosworth.

"Huh," grinned Jimmie, "guess we can unflood it. I could do it myself with a good big shovel."

"I presume the Indians will change the course

of the outlet as soon as they find some willing to market the gold for them," suggested Ned.

"We have not the least intention in the world of robbing the Indians of all the wealth," Mr. Bosworth declared. "On the contrary, we'll get the gold out and give them a fair share of the proceeds of the mine. After dinner, we'll go up and negotiate with them."

"I hope you'll send me back to New York immediately," pleaded Gilroy, turning to his employer.

"We'll all be going out directly," was the reply.

"Now, look here!" Jimmie declared. "We came in here for a vacation, and we've been mixed up with half-breeds, and Indians, and bears, and old Franciscan missions, built underground, and pots of gold at the rainbow's end, and a thousand other things that haven't given us much joy. Now I propose that we stay here and have our visit to the mountains out after all this mess is cleared up."

"I've got a bum arm," Harry exclaimed, "but I vote for staying in the hills a month. If I can't climb trees and send Boy Scout signals floating over the mountain tops," he added with a laugh, "I can sit here and broil bear steaks and have all the fun in the world seeing you boys eating them. That will be fun enough for me!"

"Besides," he went on with an amusing grin, "I want to stay here long enough to make the personal acquaintance of that flag on the cliff— the flag of Spain, without any yellow in it, that stands for a billion of yellow metal not far away!"

"The flag on the cliff?" repeated Mr. Bosworth.

"Sure," replied Jimmie. "There has been a stone flag waving on the cliff over the old mine for two or three hundred years. It isn't much of a flag to look at, but it represents the kingdom of Spain, crown and all, and the old Indians loved it because they knew of the treasure it guarded."

"Then our first visit," Mr. Bosworth declared, "shall be to the flag on the cliff!"

## CHAPTER XXII

### A FIGHT IN THE AIR

"My idea of a pleasant afternoon," Ned said, as they arose from a sumptuous camp dinner, "is to get off alone into the mountains. Mr. Bosworth seems inclined to go with you boys for a view of the flag on the cliff," he went on, "and so I'll leave you to your own amusement while I go and get acquainted with the mountains."

"You would better come with us, and see what's going on at the Devil's Punch Bowl," Jimmie advised.

"Somehow, ever since I've been here," Ned went on with a smile, "I have lived in an atmosphere of excitement. We shall be leaving the mountains before long, and I have a notion that I'd like to get up to the snow line and look over the country."

"I should think you'd had enough of the snow line at the Devil's Punch Bowl!" Frank laughed.

"That wasn't the real snow line," Ned replied. "It was pretty cold up there, it is true, but still we didn't get to the real thing."

"I should like very much to go with you,"

Mr. Bosworth suggested, "only my time is limited, and I really must investigate this mine about which so much has been said."

The result of this conversation was that Frank, Jack and Norman started away with Mr. Bosworth, leaving Harry and Gilroy at the camp, while Ned turned straight west and pointed for an elevation which seemed to be something like 10,000 feet above sea level.

The boy's days and nights for a long time had been filled with adventure, and now he was more than pleased to be away from all hostile influences. The way was not difficult for a time, and he walked along taking great draughts of mountain air and feasting his eyes on the wonderful landscape to the east.

About three o'clock in the afternoon he came to a cliff from which, through a break in the chain of mountains, he could look out toward the Pacific. The slope toward the sea was more gradual there, and the boy gazed over valleys in the great chain with feelings of awe in his heart.

As he stood on the cliff looking out to the west, he caught sight of an eagle perched on a crag not far above him.

"It wouldn't be a bad idea," the boy thought, "to take back an eagle as a trophy. Boy Scouts as a rule," he reasoned with himself, "are not supposed to take the life of any wild creatures for their own amusement or benefit. Still, I never saw anything about an eagle that looked very patriotic, or very much in touch with the softer side of animal life. The eagle, notwithstanding its prominence on the American dollar, is merely a bird of prey, eating its game alive and killing out of pure viciousness."

The great bird finally left the crag and swung nearer and nearer to the place where Ned stood. The boy crouched down behind a boulder and watched it with no little interest.

"I don't suppose it is the right thing to do," Ned mused, as he drew his automatic revolver, "but I just naturally want that eagle in the Boy Scout club room in New York. The boys of the Eagle Patrol would greet him with an ovation which he will never receive while alive."

When the eagle came nearer, the boy fired. The huge monarch of the air fell at the base of the cliff, shot through the heart.

"Now, thought the boy," looking down in dismay, "how am I ever going to get him. It doesn't seem to me that any human being can descend this precipice."

After studying the lay of the country for some moments, Ned decided to at least make an attempt to reach the eagle. Removing his coat, and leaving his revolver and searchlight upon the ledge as too cumbersome to carry, he started down toward where the bird lay. He had indeed reached the snow line, for the crevices in the wall down which he clambered were filled with frost. It was a long, long journey down to the ledge below, and dangerous, too, but the boy finally succeeded in reaching the spot where the eagle lay.

It was a noble bird, something like seven feet from tip to tip, and Ned realized that he would have his hands full in conveying it to the shelf where he had very foolishly left his coat and his weapon.

"I must have been out of my head to leave the articles there!" he exclaimed, annoyed at his own reckless act. "Now," he went on, "I've got to climb back up that almost perpendicular wall and get there before dark, too. If I had only brought the things with me the way to camp would be easier."

After several attempts to climb the wall of rock, Ned was brought to the conclusion that the feat was impossible. The downward climb had been difficult, but the return was out of the question. After a further study of the situation, he passed along the ledge to a slope which seemed to him to lead to the shelf above. In ten minutes, he found to his dismay that the slope did not connect with the shelf he sought.

However, the only thing for him to do was to proceed on the way he had chosen, in the hope that some arrangement of surfaces would permit of his return to the point where he had left the articles mentioned.

At last he came to a narrow shelf of rock in front of which was a straight fall of hundreds of feet. Above him the crag rose to a height almost as great. The shelf was not more than two feet in width, and there were places where the rock had crumbled away so that the breadth was cut down to less than six inches.

Very much disgusted with his own thoughtlessness, Ned turned toward a slope to the east and tried to make his way off the dangerous elevation. As he did so, he heard a whir of wings and felt fanning pinions brush his back.

Turning he saw two huge eagles hovering in the air hardly a yard away. Their vicious eyes were fixed angrily upon him. Involuntarily the boy reached for his revolver but, of course, did not find it in its usual place. It reposed on the shelf hundreds of feet away!

"Now," thought the boy, "I seem to be having the quiet little communion with nature I set out to attain! If these eagles actually attack me here, unarmed as I am, I'm afraid there'll be somebody falling over the precipice in a short time."

While these thoughts were passing through the excited mind of the boy, the eagles, after taking a long swing in the air, approached him, claws and beak threatening destruction.

It was a peculiar situation. Ned was still standing on a ledge a little more than a foot wide, entirely unarmed except for a large knife which he carried in his pocket. It seemed to him that a battle with the birds there could result in only one way.

He did not entirely abandon hope, but he knew that the chances were against him. It seemed that one powerful stroke from a wing must send him over the precipice.

He drew his knife from his pocket and opened it. He was not a moment too soon, for at that instant one of the eagles slashed at him with a beak which seemed to the boy at that time to be something like three feet in length. Threatened with the knife, the bird flew away, but his mate immediately continued the attack.

While obliged to meet only one bird at a time, Ned succeeded admirably in fighting them off, but directly they both charged at the same instant, and then Ned felt the powerful beaks tearing at his hands, at his legs and at his head. By keeping the blade of his knife flashing constantly before his face, he was able to protect himself when the eagles dashed at his eyes!

More than once he was thrown to the ledge by the fanning of great wings which seemed to the boy to be operated by sixty-horse power motors. Time after time he lay almost at the very verge of the precipice. Fighting desperately with knife and feet, however, he managed to escape the claws of the great birds.

Had either one of them succeeded in fastening those powerful weapons upon the boy, he must have been dragged from the ledge. During all this struggle the birds had been wounded time and again, but no fatal blow had been dealt, and so they fought on as if determined to avenge the death of their companion.

It seemed to Ned that the battle lasted for several hours. As a matter of fact, it was over in twenty minutes. A fortunate blow with the knife crippled one of the wings of the fiercest eagle so that he fluttered away into the canon, unable to lift his body to the attack again. The second bird fought more warily after this, but the boy received several wounds and several blows from his fanning wings before a knife thrust in the throat sent the vicious bird tumbling into the space below.

Freed from his assailants, the boy dropped on the ledge and panted for breath. Every muscle had been strained to its utmost tension in the encounter, and, besides, the boy had been cruelly wounded by his antagonists of the air.

He lay there resting for some moments and then, rising, found it necessary to cut his shirt into ribbons in order to bind up some of the wounds which had been inflicted and from which the blood was trickling in considerable quantities.

"Talk about the great American eagle!" mused the boy. "I shall never want to see one again unless he's on a piece of money! The noble bird of liberty is certainly a scrapper when it comes down to brass tacks, but the encounter of today shows that he is inclined to take every advantage of an opponent!"

Regarding his torn clothes ruefully, the boy once more glanced up at the shelf where he had very foolishly deposited his coat, his revolver and flashlight. His hat had been torn from his head during the first minute of the battle.

"It strikes me," he considered, "that I'd better head for camp without going back after that plunder."

Through the break in the mountainous range in which he stood he could see the red sun dropping low down into the sky. He knew that to attempt to secure his property would be to give up all hope of reaching camp before the night fell.

The next question for him to consider was as to whether he should attempt to convey the bird he had shot into camp.

"If I don't take in the prize," he mused with a smile showing on his face, "the boys will pretend to believe that I never had any battle with an eagle; that I received my injuries in some other way."

He looked down at his torn clothing and at his bandaged wrists, and for a moment, realizing how tired he was, resolved to abandon the prize for the time being and make for the camp at all speed. At last, however, the boy's indomitable courage asserted itself, and he picked up the heavy bird and started on his journey to camp.

Somehow the conformation of the land seemed to always lead him away from the direction he hoped to follow. Here a ledge he was following wound sharply around to the south, ending in a precipitous slope which obliged him to retrace his steps. There a gully in the hills threw a mountain torrent in his path. Long before he saw the light of the campfire, he was nearly ready to drop from exhaustion.

The cheerful blaze, however, brought new courage to his heart and before long he came within the circle of light. When he turned the angle of the rock, Harry and Gilroy greeted him with exclamations of dismay.

## CHAPTER XXIII

### THE TREATY UNDER THE FLAG

"My dear sir!" exclaimed Gilroy as Ned, hatless, coatless, ragged, and well covered with blood, advanced into the firelight.

"Now, what do you think of that!" exclaimed Harry.

Ned dropped down on the ground and turned a tired face to the others.

"What do you think of a battle in the air?" he asked.

"Not up in the air, really?" asked Gilroy.

"We had battles in the air when we were running our aeroplanes," commented Harry, "and we rather liked them!"

"This little encounter," Ned explained, "was with a great American eagle, or eagles, rather. The eagle is a scrapper!"

As he spoke he pointed to the body of the dead bird laying just outside the illuminated circle. Gilroy hastened in that direction, but paused when a flutter of wind caused the feathers of the bird to move threateningly.

"Is it alive?" he asked.

"Harry lifted the bird by the neck and drew it nearer to the flame.

"This eagle," he said with a grin, " is about the deadest thing I ever saw.   In fact," he went on, "he is fully as dead as the eagle on a counterfeit dollar!"

"Where did you get it?" asked Gilroy.

"I fought for it," answered Ned.

"I know what's the matter with Ned," Harry exclaimed.   "He hasn't had anything to eat since noon, and he's hungry.   Never try to talk to a Boy Scout when he's hungry," he continued, "if you do, you'll get saucy answers."

"I'm hungry myself!" Gilroy declared.

"Well," Harry answered.   "You can get supper any old time you want to.   I'd be glad to serve as chef tonight if it wasn't for this bum old arm.   I could do a pretty good job cooking with one hand, only I'm just a little bit weak yet."

Gilroy at once accepted the invitation and began preparations for supper, going about the work awkwardly.

"What are you going to have for supper?" he asked after a survey of the provision shelves.

"Bear stew!" laughed Harry, well knowing the fat clerk's abhorrence of bear flesh.   "We're all going to eat bear stew.   But you can have a broiled rattlesnake if you care to go and catch one."

Gilroy threw up his hands in horror.

"Do you eat rattlesnakes, really?" he asked.

Ned and Harry joined in a laugh at sight of the clerk's disturbed countenance. After a time Ned arose to assist in the preparation of the meal, and then, for the first time, the others took note of the absence of his coat and hat.

"Where are they?" Harry asked, pointing from breast to head.

Then Ned explained his plight and Gilroy shuddered in sympathy.

"On a narrow ledge," he wailed, "hundreds of feet up in the air, a battle with two great birds like that! I've heard a great deal about the Pacific coast," he went on, "and have long desired a trip like the present one, but I'll tell you now that my infatuation for the west has vanished. Now I begin to understand," he continued, "why we rarely see a very old man west of Denver."

"What becomes of 'em?" asked Harry.

"They are eaten by bears, and scalped by Indians, and drowned in places like the Devil's Punch Bowl, and chewed up by eagles, and slaughtered by half-breeds!" replied the clerk. "And the wonder of it all is," he continued, "that they seem to like it!"

When the stew was simmering merrily on the coals and the coffee was bubbling not far away, Ned began bringing out the dishes and clearing away the litter of the fire.

"I suppose," he said after a time, "that the others will be back for supper.  It seems to me that they are making a long trip to the Devil's Punch Bowl."

"I know why they're staying away such a long time," Harry cut in, with a grin.  "They're up on top of the mountain waving the stone flag on the cliff.  That's a cheerful job, too."

"My dear sir!" almost gasped Gilroy.  "My information is to the effect that the flag on the cliff is really carved out of stone!"

"It certainly is carved out of stone," Ned answered.  "In any other event it would have come to an ignoble end long ago."

"Who carved it there?" asked Harry.

"I have no information on the subject," Ned replied, "except what common sense gives me. The mine under the mountain was undoubtedly discovered and worked by the Hoola Indians who first inhabited this country.  Later on, the Franciscans came here and established their mission. Still later, the Spaniards came and claimed to own the country.

"It is my opinion," he went on, "that the flag was carved there to stand as a lasting monument to Spain two or three hundred years ago. Probably the Hoola Indians, whose titles to the lands were recognized by the Spanish and Mexican governments, chose that form of a monument to indicate the location of the mine."

"And so," Harry exclaimed, "that stone flag has waved above millions in gold for hundreds of years, and no one knew the significance of it—no one except the Hoola Indians."

"That's the way it seems to me!" Ned answered.

Just as the coffee and the stew were ready for consumption, Jimmie came dashing into the camp, closely followed by the others, with Mr. Bosworth, unfamiliar with mountain work, puffing along in the rear.

"Mother of Moses!" cried Jimmie. "I smelled that stew away up on the snow line!"

"And I got a whiff of the coffee from the edge of the Devil's Punch Bowl," laughed Jack.

Then Jimmie caught sight of Ned's disheveled appearance and began a critical examination of the tears in his garments and his wounds.

"You look," the boy laughed, "like you'd been in a rough house at Coney Island. Where did you get it?"

Mr. Bosworth now came up, and, with all

present, the story of the battle in the air was again told.

"And you left your gun and your searchlight and your coat up in the blue sky, did you?" demanded Jimmie.

"I certainly did," replied Ned. "But you step over to the barrier and see what I brought back to represent them."

Jimmie did as requested and soon came back into the firelight, dragging the dead eagle.

"That's some bird!" he chuckled. "Say, Ned," he went on in a moment. "I know where you can get all kinds of money for that. The Sioux Indians will give a dollar apiece for the feathers for their hair."

"This bird goes to the Eagle Patrol, New York," Ned declared.

"Good for you!" shouted Jimmie. "We'll hang it up in the club room and give you a seat of honor directly under it."

"I beg your pardon," Gilroy interrupted, "but if its all the same to you, Mr. Bosworth, and to you boys, I'd like to partake of a little refreshment. This mountain air certainly does bring about an appetite!"

"I knew that something was giving me an appetite," grinned Jimmie, "but I didn't know what it was!"

"Cripes!" Jack laughed. "Jimmie had just

the same kind of an appetite on the Amazon!''

"And Jimmie's got just the same kind of an appetite now, too!'' replied the boy, ladling out a great dish of stew. "I'm going to devour just three portions like this!'' he insisted.

"Now, boys,'' Mr. Bosworth said after supper was well under day, "I feel obliged to start for New York tomorrow, taking Gilroy with me.''

"Don't you do it!'' cried Jimmie. "We won't have any fun if Gilroy goes away!''

"And my advice to you,'' the lawyer went on, "is to come along with me.''

"Oh, Dad!'' cried Jack. "Just because you got your business all in shape you want to drag us off to New York.''

"I'm only giving advice,'' Mr. Bosworth replied, with a smile. "You boys can do just as you please.''

"Glory be!'' shouted Jack.

"Have you really completed your business here?'' asked Ned in a moment.

"Yes,'' was the reply.

"Satisfactorily?'' asked Ned.

"Entirely so! You see,'' the lawyer went on, "my theory is always to work along the lines of least resistance. I understand, of course, that we could establish our claim to these lands through the courts. I understand, too, that the Hoola Indians who claim title could be electrocuted for the murder of Toombs. That would clear the atmosphere of many complications."

"But it wouldn't be right!" Jimmie shouted.

"No, it wouldn't be right," Mr. Bosworth admitted. "The Indians really have some rights here which should be respected, and Toombs received only his just deserts. He never had any standing, even in Wall street. He has betrayed every confidence for years, and there is not a soul on earth who will mourn his death."

"That's the way I sized him up!" Ned said.

"And so, taking all things into consideration," Mr. Bosworth went on, "I have decided to give the Indians a fair price for their land—more than enough to keep them in luxury the remainder of their lives—and to employ them to direct the taking out of the gold."

"Is there a lot of it?" asked Jack.

"It seems," Mr. Bosworth replied. "that the eight Indians now living mined the gold secretly until a few years ago, when, believing that they had enough for all their future needs, they turned the waters of the pool into the mine. At this time they had large stores of the precious metal in an interior chamber, where one of their number was always kept on guard."

"I think I had a peep into that chamber!" Jack exclaimed.

"So far as I can understand, the treasure chamber is the one you boys saw," Mr. Bosworth went on, "and you were lucky to get out alive, too," he added. "Only the arrival of Ned and Jimmie protected you."

"That's more than Toombs did—get out alive!" Jimmie suggested.

"When, at some time in the near future, the water is turned back into the other channel," Mr. Bosworth said, "the body of Toombs will be taken out and given reverent and decent burial. That is all that can be done for him now. His companions in New York will never know his fate."

The boys sat by the campfire late that night, discussing plans and occasionally referring some disputed point to Mr. Bosworth.

"Why, lads," laughed the lawyer, "I've given you my best advice, and that is that you take your vacation in some less dangerous locality. However, if you won't follow my line of thought, my next best advice is for you to remain in this camp and breathe mountain air, and hunt squirrels, and deer, and bear, for a month and then return to New York."

"Think of a person remaining here when he might go back to the big city!" exclaimed Gilroy. "Why," he continued, "the half-breeds are likely to break out again at any moment."

"The half-breeds deserted when Huga was killed," Norman replied. "They were brought here on day wages, and will never show up again."

"And what are we going to do with Norman?" asked Jack, his attention called to the boy by the remark.

"Bring him back to New York with you," replied Mr. Bosworth, "and I will take pleasure in looking after his future, also that of his sister."

"Bully for you, Dad!" Jack exclaimed.

"I'll get him a job on Dad's paper as a reporter," Frank promised.

"That's just the thing!" exclaimed Norman.

The party passed a restful night, and early in the morning Mr. Bosworth and Gilroy set out for the return trip. As they had made no arrangements for guides or teams, the boys accompanied them until, from far up on the mountainside, they saw the roofs of a little town from which telegrams asking for horses might be sent.

As the two descended the slope, the boys waved their handkerchiefs in farewell and promised to show up in New York within a month.

"And we'll do it, too!" Ned declared as they set their faces toward their camp.

"We'll be in New York if we ain't having too much fun here!" Jimmie laughed.

During the following month the boys enjoyed their vacation to the fullest. They slept out on the range, hunted and fished in the cold mountain rivers, and had, as Jimmie always expressed it, the time of their lives. They were back in New York on time ready for the next adventure which might come in their way.

The presentation of the eagle to the Eagle Patrol was the sensation of the year among the Boy Scouts of New York. To this day, it occupies the place of honor in the club room, having been mounted by one of the most famous taxidermists of the city.

Mr. Bosworth fulfilled his promise to look after the future of Norman and his sister, and they were soon placed at work, much to their liking with prospects of happy lives before them.

Months afterward, when the employes of the corporation represented by Mr. Bosworth, gathered near the old Spanish Mission and the Devil's Punch Bowl to remove the treasure of gold from the mine, there was some talk among them of the strange hieroglyphics carved high up on the smooth surface of the rocks.

"I don't know what it all means," the superintendent of the company said, "but while I was in New York, talking with Mr. Bosworth,

I often heard that peculiar formation referred to. Now," he added thoughtfully, "what was it they called it. Ah! I know," he added, his eyes brightening. "They called it THE FLAG ON THE CLIFF."

The End

**ALWAYS** *ASK FOR THE* **DONOHUE**
Complete Editions and you will get the best for the least money

# Henty Series

## *FOR BOYS*

G. A. Henty was the most prolific writer of boy's stories of the nineteenth century. From two to five books a year came from his facile pen. No Christmas holidays were complete without a new "Henty Book." This new series comprises 45 titles. They are printed on an extra quality of paper, from new plates and bound in the best quality of cloth, stamped on back and side in inks from unique and attractive dies. 12 mo. cloth. Each book in a printed wrapper.

| | | | |
|---|---|---|---|
| 1 | Among Malay Pirates | 24 | Lion of St. Mark |
| 2 | Bonnie Prince Charlie | 25 | Lion of the North |
| 3 | Boy Knight, The | 26 | Lost Heir, The |
| 4 | Bravest of the Brave | 27 | Maori and Settler |
| 5 | By England's Aid | 28 | One of the 28th |
| 6 | By Pike and Dyke | 29 | Orange and Green |
| 7 | By Right of Conquest | 30 | Out on the Pampas |
| 8 | By Sheer Pluck | 31 | Queen's Cup, The |
| 9 | Captain Bayley's Heir | 32 | Rujub, the Juggler |
| 10 | Cat of Bubastes | 33 | St. George for England |
| 11 | Col. Thorndyke's Secret | 34 | Sturdy and Strong |
| 12 | Cornet of Horse, The | 35 | Through the Fray |
| 13 | Dragon and the Raven | 36 | True to the Old Flag |
| 14 | Facing Death | 37 | Under Drake's Flag |
| 15 | Final Reckoning, A | 38 | With Clive in India |
| 16 | For Name and Fame | 39 | With Lee in Virginia |
| 17 | For the Temple | 40 | With Wolfe in Canada |
| 18 | Friends, Though Divided | 41 | Young Buglers, The |
| 19 | Golden Canon | 42 | Young Carthaginians |
| 20 | In Freedom's Cause | 43 | Young Colonists, The |
| 21 | In the Reign of Terror | 44 | Young Franc-Tireurs |
| 22 | In Times of Peril | 45 | Young Midshipman |
| 23 | Jack Archer | | |

All of above titles can be procured at the store where this book was bought, or sent to any address for 50c. postage paid, by the publishers

## M. A. DONOHUE & CO.,

**701-727 South Dearborn Street  -  -  CHICAGO**

# BOYS' COPYRIGHTED BOOKS

The most attractive and highest class list of copyrighted books for boys ever printed. In this list will be found the works of W. Bert Foster, Capt. Ralph Bonehill, Arthur M. Winfield, etc.

Printed from large clear type, illustrated, bound in a superior quality of cloth.

## THE CLINT WEBB SERIES
### By W. Bert Foster

1.—Swept Out to Sea; or, Clint Webb Among the Whalers.
2.—The Frozen Ship; or, Clint Webb Among the Sealers.
3.—From Sea to Sea; or, Clint Webb on the Windjammer.
4.—The Sea Express; or, Clint Webb and the Sea Tramp.

## THE YOUNG SPORTSMAN'S SERIES
### By Capt. Ralph Bonehill

Rival Cyclists; or, Fun and Adventures on the Wheel.
Young Oarsmen of Lake View; or, The Mystery of Hermit Island.
Leo the Circus Boy; or, Life Under the Great White Canvas.

## SEA AND LAND SERIES
### Four Boys' Books by Favorite Authors

Oscar the Naval Cadet......................Capt. Ralph Bonehill
Blue Water Rovers..........................Victor St. Clare
A Royal Smuggler...........................William Dalton
A Boy Crusoe...............................Allen Erie

## ADVENTURE AND JUNGLE SERIES
### A large, well printed, attractive edition.

Guy in the Jungle..........................Wm. Murray Grayden
Casket of Diamonds.........................Oliver Optic
The Boy Railroader ........................Matthew White, Jr.
Treasure of South Lake Farm...............W. Bert Foster

## YOUNG HUNTERS SERIES
### By Capt. Ralph Bonehill

Gun and Sled; or, The Young Hunters of Snow Top Island.
Young Hunters in Porto Rico; or, The Search for a Lost Treasure.
Two Young Crusoes; by C. W. Phillips.
Through Apache Land; or, Ned in the Mountains; by Lieut. R. H. Tayne.

## BRIGHT AND BOLD SERIES
### By Arthur M. Winfield

Poor but Plucky; or, The Mystery of a Flood.
School Days of Fred Harley; or, Rivals for All Honors.
By Pluck, not Luck; or, Dan Granbury's Struggle to Rise.
The Missing Tin Box; or, Hal Carson's Remarkable City Adventure.

## COLLEGE LIBRARY FOR BOYS
### By Archdeacon Farrar

Julian Home; or, A Tale of College Life.
St. Winifred's; or, The World of School.

For sale by all booksellers, or sent postpaid on receipt of 50 cents.

## M. A. DONOHUE & CO.

701-723 So. Dearborn Street,　　　　　　　　Chicago

# BOYS' COPYRIGHTED BOOKS

Printed from large, clear type on a superior quality of paper, embellished with original illustrations by eminent artists, and bound in a superior quality of book binders' cloth, ornamented with illustrated covers, stamped in colors from unique and appropriate dies, each book wrapped in a glazed paper wrapper printed in colors.

## MOTOR BOAT BOYS SERIES
### By Louis Arundel

1.—The Motor Club's Cruise Down the Mississippi; or, The Dash for Dixie.
2.—The Motor Club on the St. Lawrence River; or, Adventures Among the Thousand Islands.
3.—The Motor Club on the Great Lakes; or, Exploring the Mystic Isle of Mackinac.
4.—Motor Boat Boys Among the Florida Keys; or, The Struggle for the Leadership.
5.—Motor Boat Boys Down the Coast; or, Through Storm and Stress.
6.—Motor Boat Boys' River Chase.

## THE BIRD BOYS SERIES
### By John Luther Langworthy

1.—The Bird Boys; or, The Young Sky Pilots' First Air Voyage.
2.—The Bird Boys on the Wing; or, Aeroplane Chums in the Tropics.
3.—The Bird Boys Among the Clouds; or, Young Aviators in a Wreck.
4.—Bird Boys' Flight; or, A Hydroplane Round-up.
5.—Bird Boys' Aeroplane Wonder; or, Young Aviators on a Cattle Ranch.

## CANOE AND CAMPFIRE SERIES
### By St. George Rathborne

1.—Canoe Mates in Canada; or, Three Boys Afloat on the Saskatchewan.
2.—Young Fur Takers; or, Traps and Trails in the Wilderness.
3.—The House Boat Boys; or, Drifting Down to the Sunny South.
4.—Chums in Dixie; or, The Strange Cruise in the Motor Boat.
5.—Camp Mates in Michigan; or, With Pack and Paddle in the Pine Woods.
6.—Rocky Mountain Boys; or, Camping in the Big Game Country.

---

For sale by all booksellers, or sent postpaid on receipt of 50 cents.

**M. A. DONOHUE & CO.**

**701–733 So. Dearborn Street,**        **Chicago**